Disciples of Passion

Middle East Literature in Translation

Michael Beard *and* Adnan Haydar, *Series Editors*

Hoda Barakat

DISCIPLES
of PASSION

Translated from the Arabic by Marilyn Booth

SYRACUSE UNIVERSITY PRESS

Syracuse University Press
Syracuse, New York 13244–5160

First Edition 2005
05 06 07 08 09 10   6 5 4 3 2 1

Previously published in Arabic as *Ahl al-Hawa* (Beirut: Dar al-Nahar, 1993).

The paper used in this publication meets the minimum requirements of American
National Standard for Information Science—Permanence of Paper for Printed
Library Materials, ANSI Z39.48–1984.∞™

Library of Congress Cataloging-in-Publication Data

Barakāt, Hudā.
[Ahl al-hawā. English]
Disciples of passion / Hoda Barakat ; translated from the Arabic by Marilyn Booth.
p. cm.—(Middle East literature in translation)
ISBN 0–8156–0833–0 (alk. paper)
I. Booth, Marilyn. II. Title. III. Series.
PJ7816.A672A6413 2005
892.7'36—dc22   2005018501

Manufactured in the United States of America

Contents

Hoda Barakat, author of four novels and an earlier short story collection, has lived in Paris since 1989, after leaving Lebanon during that country's long civil war. She received her bachelor's degree in French literature from the Lebanese University in 1974. She has worked as a teacher, researcher, print and broadcast journalist, and information director for Radio Orient. Among the prizes she has won is the Naguib Mahfouz Prize for her novel *The Tiller of Waters,* also translated by Marilyn Booth. Her fourth novel, *Sayyidi wa-habibi,* came out in Beirut in December 2004.

Marilyn Booth is associate professor in the Program in Comparative and World Literature at the University of Illinois, Urbana-Champaign. She has translated numerous works of fiction and memoir from the Arabic, including *Leaves of Narcissus,* by Somaya Ramadan; *The Open Door,* by Latifa al-Zayyat; the prize-winning *Points of the Compass* by Sahar Tawfiq; and *My Grandmother's Cactus: Stories by Egyptian Women.* Her most recent critical book is *May Her Likes Be Multiplied: Biography and Gender Politics in Egypt* (2001); her current project focuses on aesthetics and historicity in early Arabic feminist writing.

Disciples of Passion

Part One

1

After killing her, I sat down on a high boulder.

I closed my eyes for a long spell, keeping them shut until my breathing was calm and regular. My joints went slack, and I felt my limbs and organs flow together like waters commingling after their pent-up energies have surged toward the point of collision. Now that I had reclaimed it, my skin was softly cool in the mild and pleasant breeze. Now I had retrieved my protective shell, strong and seamless, unbroken by cracks or punctures. New.

I lay full length on the boulder. It felt so soft, yielding to me like a downy mattress, following the angles of my body and settling compliantly around them. I opened my eyes upon an enormous moon, low in the sky. Tonight the heavens were a dark indigo, swollen with sharp, young stars. Their abundance filled the heavens: intensely bright sparks of light, as if they had that moment exploded into being. The sky was fresh, almost raw, and so near, exactly as I remembered it from childhood. If I were to reach out a hand, I would touch it, of that I was sure . . . so sure that I did not even bother to try. What separated me from the firmament was air, only air, and such a delicate, frail barrier this air created, the air that seeped into my dilated lungs and made them a mere part of the rhythmic, remote pulse of the atmosphere.

In this hour I came into the world. I gulped the universe down, greedily; I quenched my thirst. Now, I knew, I had begun to possess what I had been seeking as long as I'd been alive. Now, I thought: only now do I occupy my own being, the whole of it; I own this self of mine that has flowed into space to become a fragment of it. It is as if I am giving birth to myself. I give myself, my soul, to the wind, to the forest, to the ravines and the sky; and they tender themselves to me.

At the moment I killed her, when I saw and realized that I had killed her, I knew that I had breathed in her soul. I swallowed the angel of her, and it was within me. The sky flung itself wide before me; all of space broke open, and my body unfolded itself. A sacred being, a saint: that, I knew, was what I was. I knew that this body of mine had embarked on its slow but assured ascent. I knew that if one day they were to open my tomb, they would not find me there. They would find nothing but my shroud, split asunder, emptied; they would find only the women, tipping their scents into the soil and running, joyous, to tell the tidings of my absence.

For whosoever has not killed does not know.

Whosoever has not killed remains prey to fancies, prey to suffering, captive to an enervating search for wondrous salvation. That person's existence will be as the life of a fly at the rubbish dump, circling endlessly round the same point, inhaling indigestible, bloated questions, then and there to die without having so much as disturbed the stagnant air.

Whosoever has not known the stirrings of passion, the tensions of longing, love as fully realized as a fiery midday sun, has no knowledge at all. Full, whole, perfect is love, like a mammoth nuclear explosion that erupts once to cloud the skies forever and always. The passionless person does not know. Does not know that the seed of death finds its auspicious bed in the rank climate of darkness, at the moment when we are certain from the first touch that this is really it, this particular skin with its own warmth adjusted exceptionally and with finality to the heat of our own skin, for its sake. This is the seed of killing.

But the lust of it will never come to fruition in souls that are small. The lust of it will never reign over those inconsequential hearts that know only how to give in to illness. Withdrawing into tears, into the strains of songs, they sadly contemplate their old photographs: stunted souls they are, forever denied perfection.

Here I am, rising, to flood across the suckling world like blessed milk. I flow, never to dwindle. The flow of me may never grow meager, for I have been offered forgiveness. I have been blessed. My grace is to find the seed ripening in the moisture of my self, growing to flower and to bear fruit. And we shall pluck and eat the fruit. We shall eat the fruit; we shall enter heaven. We shall be returned unto heaven in the merit and worthiness that is our due.

Now I rise from the rock to walk, my tread so light that I almost soar. I open my arms like Yohanna and sing: I, too, have a mouth that drips gold. I chant the tidings of the Lord, the name of the Lord whom I have come to know. The Lord whom I have touched, embraced. I step forward, singing at full voice. I do not stop to turn back, to look behind me, to where I have left her at the cairn of stones. There is no need, for I know that she is no longer there. She is within me, or if she is not, then she has risen into the heavens.

Dawn, almost here. The rooftops of the hamlets in the facing mountains reveal themselves in the glow, though still submerged in the purplish droplets of a sleepy dawn. I sing and sing, loud and high, to the sun that will rise for me, to flood me in its vehement heat.

2

A spotted cow, brown on white.

No. It's a reddish brown cow. A reddish brown cow grazing in a vast green plain. The grass is cropped very short on this level land, and nothing else breaks the line of the horizon, not even trees or a lake's surface to reflect the intensely blue sky.

Afternoon. Late afternoon, for the sun is already dipping westward. Now and then the cow lows, long, languidly. She gives her head a shake and returns to her stolid pose, her gaze fixed on the grass in the distance.

It is all there: but none of it really exists.

Except that this peacefulness, this sense of well-being that fills me, brings alive the image of the cow in the plain. As well as anything can, its reality expresses the way I feel in the calmness of this place.

The garden here is spacious and very large, but it contains many twisting paths and hidden corners. No matter which of its many wooden benches you select, you will be able to see only small segments of this garden at any one time as it winds among the buildings and around them, joining each structure to the others through the planted spaces that separate them. Paved walks and pathways, marked out by pebbles and flowering plants, send their tentacles creeping throughout the garden to its very ends. Utterly smooth, the surfaces have been carefully planed to ease the wheelchairs' way, for they must not bump or shake their fragile burdens, so swift to bruise.

No matter where I stand, I will not truly see the walls that encircle and wholly contain this place because these outer walls of ours are not very high. From the outside, though, passersby on the main road see only the upper stories of the buildings. When you are in here, the wall shows itself only if you walk quite close to the stones themselves, most of which are covered in moss that has grown in the thick shadows cast along the wall by the towering trees clinging there.

Through all of those years in which the city's trees and wooded parks were strafed by repeated bombing until finally they burned, the tall trees here remained tall, towering over the walls. Our little rise (covered—even now—in a fresh and vigorous green) abuts that city. Dayr al-Salib, the Cloisters of the Cross, as our little hill submerged in radiant green is called, was one of the areas most badly hit. Yet the hospital was preserved by the Lord (as the Sisters say) and with an impervious insistence. Unlike the other hospitals in our country, it stayed comfortably afloat on the waters of the Lord's mercy, lasting throughout the whole of those long, long years. And by extraordinary coincidence, all of the combatants were in accord (with the Lord) that this place—and only this place—must keep on as it was before, that it must stay beyond the reach of all the bombing and other acts of destruction, even those of a completely arbitrary nature.

Dayr al-Salib is a hospital for nervous disorders and mental diseases. When my family despaired of me, they brought me here, grieving deeply about a condition that they did not know how to mend.

When they brought me here, I almost fainted from the shock. It surprised me, I mean, that they chose the very time in which I was feeling happier than I had ever felt in my life. They chose that moment to weep for me and to make their farewells—and in this fashion. I opened my mouth to make a loud and sobbing protest, but no words came to my rescue. No words came out that would make them understand. My sister Asmaa was crying hard, tears streaming from her eyes all the while she was speaking with the nun and kissing the enormous black cross on the nun's chest. Then my sister stepped farther away, staring at me, but not really seeing me. She didn't even try to understand the loud rattling that was rising from my throat and lungs. I was trying desperately to shape the sound into words like those I used to produce so easily, but now I could no longer recall even their rudiments. I couldn't make those basic shapes that rise from the chest to the mouth, where, saturated with moisture and filled with the energy of movement, they emerge as words. Asmaa began to sob loudly as she arranged my few belongings in the white metal armoire. I was breathing in quick, deep gulps. All I wanted was to get to the point where I could form her name and force it out of my mouth, before she could leave me here and go away. A s m a—a . . .

She was already striding down the corridor when I caught up with her, evading the many hands that were reaching for me. Still crying, she reached for the nun's hand and gripped it, hard. She paused, swiveled to look at me, and then walked on, faster. She went through the door, that massive door that closed tightly behind her before I was able to give her even the smallest sign to tell her that I felt in the best of states. Before I could tell her that I was—on this very day, precisely—a most happy person.

3

I did not have a clear sense of how much time had passed when Asmaa came to visit me for the first time. Anyway, was it really the first visit? They would leave me sleeping, all the time it seemed. When I saw her standing there in front of me, her eyes sad yet hollow, I felt very irritated with her. I stared out the window on the far side of the sitting room where they had brought me to see her. I figured out that it was still autumn, as it had been when they brought me here. So perhaps she had not stayed away from me for so very long after all. Quickly I wiped the rebuke off my face and smiled at her. She smiled back.

She took me by the hand and walked me into the garden. I studied her small hand, and then I stared at the crown of her head, which came no higher than my shoulder. Asmaa is a small person, like my father. This body of mine, though, has the bulk of my maternal grandfather.

Asmaa sat me down in the sunshine and breeze. She smiled at me steadily, but without saying anything. I became aware that the slippers on my feet were truly ugly, and I yanked them away from my cold toes. Why, I asked Asmaa, had she brought me these slippers that I hadn't even wanted? I waited for her to speak.

That visit took place on one of the days in a stretch of time when I was always forgetting where I was. Walking through the garden, I would ask people where we were. Where are we? I would say. But I never heard their answers, not even once. As long as I was in my room, I did not ask myself this question, but in the garden—once they began to allow me into the garden, that is—I would forget where I was. Then I got used to forgetting where I was, and I began to enjoy simply sitting there. And I walked. I liked to walk.

Every one of Asmaa's later visits resembled that first one. She no longer cried, though. Now she talked to me, and she brought me lots of things that were supposed to be familiar but weren't. Asmaa began to irritate me, perhaps because she seemed persuaded that I was sad or that I was determined to have everything gloomy around me; so I began to forget about her, much of the time I forgot about her, as if she were no longer my sister Asmaa. Whenever I watched her closely for any amount of time, I saw my father. I saw my father, my father; yes, I kept on seeing my father. Then I would say to her, "I want to go upstairs, I'm tired now." And Asmaa would go away.

I can see my father as he raises his hand to his ear. He clears his throat and puts his hand to his ear and closes one eye. He is about to sing in his soothing, gentle voice, the little voice that is so like him.

Our house, in these moments, would be crowded with people, but however many there were, everyone would grow quiet as soon as he called out his familiar "ooof." They would set down their tiny glasses of *arak,* their faces taking on an expression of profound satisfaction as they nodded their heads and replied with their own "ooof." Ooof, ooof. . . .

I try to put my hand to my ear, just so, but I find it hard to do because my head is weak, and it topples every which way, and I just cannot keep it steady. I have to put my entire weight behind it, all the heaviness of my enormous body. I brace my head with all the parts of my body, all the parts helping out as if they are the cushions of a firm sofa. But still my head floats like a cork bobbing above my spine or twists limply as if it's been set onto the neck of a newborn baby. Often my head drops into my hands, and then I just leave it there, bent crooked, even though sometimes it hurts so much that the pain seems almost to rip apart the bones at the base of my neck. I leave it like that, anyway, because after a while it all goes numb, and I can forget about it. I regain my warmth and my balance, and then I feel relaxed enough.

Sometimes I stick my head into my armpit or between my knees, and I arch my body over it, hoping that the fluids from my organs will flow into its emptiness, filling it with strength and keeping it from falling every which way. I know that before long my head will grow quiet and still. I will set about rocking it gently, trying to adjust my whole body to a single rhythm that suits it. Little by little I can make my movements more precise and regular, like the heavy pendulum of a clock. I regulate the beat even more with my voice. It rises from my body, rolled up like the tight petals of a new rose, like a water lily, calmly rising and falling on the gentle waves of my voice. My voice floats upward from all parts of my body to gather in my throat and then returns to roam within me. I want to sing, like my father. I use my whole body: I put all of it firmly to my ear, and it seems to me then that I am singing like my father. When that feeling comes to me, my irritation falls away. And I no longer forget, no longer give in to those long and frequent spells of oblivion. But my voice does not please anyone. My voice makes everyone around me nervous and agitated, to the point where the nurses come in to untie me and to make me be quiet.

In the beginning I resisted them. My body was very strong, very large and audacious. In moments of anger it would fly up into the air and circle above them like a hawk. If I so much as gave one of them a jab of my elbow, he might well fall down unconscious, some distance from me. I would stand over him, stunned by the spectacle of my own force. After calming down, I would refuse to believe it. I just couldn't accept my own strength. Where had that great strength been hiding, I asked myself, that lightness and ease with which I moved the parts of my body, as heavy as they were? Faced with my bodily strength, the male nurses—who seemed so fond and affectionate whenever they gave me baths—were infuriated, always. They rushed on me, every one of them angry, hitting me because they had been taken unawares at the force in my huge but lanky frame. They tackled me, hard, as if they really despised me, although I knew they didn't hate me. I would howl and lash out, striking at them again and again until I was too exhausted to move, until my joints loosened and my body went limp. It had to happen only a few times, though. Soon enough, when it started, I would crumple after a few minutes, long before I came close to reaching that state of bliss that meant real fatigue and a feeling of simply fading away. Once I realized that the inevitable result of all this would be another injection, I put strict limits on the pleasure of exercising my own strength. I always stopped myself before they could bring in the needle. What I don't understand, though, is why they would go on beating me for a while afterward. They didn't hate me. They just hated my voice and my strength. And maybe they didn't like it that in my illness I was there among them, upright. They could not accept that from me.

"I am not sick," I said to Asmaa. "Take me home." But many days had passed before I said those words to her, and, anyway, it took me many days to see that I had indeed grown very calm and quiet. After all, now they were leaving me alone to wander wherever I wanted. Everyone teased me and joked with me; the men who worked as nurses there were always thumping and tweaking me. They pinched me on the buttocks or reached out, laughing, to touch my sex. When

I moved quickly to hide it with both hands, they said to me, "Why hide from us? There isn't anything there now—it fell off." Then I would laugh, too, because I knew they were only playing around with me. I laughed with them.

By this time I felt little affection for Asmaa. I started to find her visits too frequent and sensed uncomfortably that her standard show of concern was exaggerated. Hardly would I see her off before she was back again, it seemed, and I repeated the same words every time. "I am not sick, Asmaa. Take me home." Her only response was that vacuous smile, so in the end I stopped saying anything.

◆   ◆   ◆

As Asmaa got older, she came to seem repugnant to me. What always struck me most about her face was her black mustache. So why, I asked myself, would I want to leave this place to go and live with Asmaa?

I knew that I had become a tranquil man because now they left me alone nearly all day long. I wandered around just as I pleased, and when the shelling began, they even asked me to help them carry the sick and take supplies down to the shelter—that is, to the basement that occupied half the area of the building. I helped them to get the shelter ready after the number of inmates grew. Those who were likely to create a disturbance had a large room to themselves. We would lay them out there after giving them injections to calm them down and put them to sleep.

On those nights when the missiles flew, our evenings were not particularly grim. It was just that we were afraid of each other; I think perhaps we were more scared of each other than of the fierce sounds of the explosions that opened up our heads to hysteria and screaming even though we had swallowed those red pills. As the candles sitting high on the little shelves sent their light through the red-hot grilles, they cast shadows that transformed our features completely, and that's why we were so afraid of each other. But in spite of our mutual fear we all tended to scuttle into one corner of the room, to huddle there in a single heap of bodies. Perhaps it was because we got so chilled at night. The shelter was very damp, and even wool blankets did not protect us from the cold after the hospital directors closed down all of the generators that kept our lights on and our buildings heated. Of course, we had to save energy, which was running low; the whole city was undergoing a severe fuel shortage.

That was my understanding of the situation. The others, though, did not grasp it, and they often wailed and howled as we huddled in the shelter. I was able to quiet them more readily than could the nurses or the nuns. They clung to me, growing more and more attached, perhaps because I was the biggest one there or the warmest, or because they believed I was their father. Ducking in under me as if I were a great big hen, they would rub their shaven heads against me and snuffle at me like chicks, or perhaps more in the way of puppies. Like puppies, too, they would sense when the shelling was about to return to its most violent level, even though the night was perfectly quiet and we were on the point of returning to our rooms and our beds. Their eyes would bulge and their movements grow jerky, and if they had been asleep, they would wake up. Hoarse, rumbling growls would come from their throats as they scampered in all directions. And very soon the shelling would resume, the reverberations as fierce as ever.

I knew that I had become a tranquil man because I had not been so in the beginning. I saw them now, and I recognized that they did not see one another. Now, I no longer experienced the same alterations in mood, the rapid shifts from one state to another.

In the beginning I used to stay calm in the shelter. But all it took was for one of them to start screaming, and then my whole body seemed to catch fire. Suddenly the hair on my head was standing straight up, and my limbs were shuddering as if I had touched live electric wires. That staggering strength of mine would stab my body, invading it with a force that would send it spinning, like a careening ball, smashing into the wall. I would commence howling and knocking my head against the wall until it exploded and I heard a deep, staccato ringing that rose to overwhelm the noise of the falling bombs. The ringing sound rose and rose to wipe out all other sounds, replacing them, submerging them in the pleasure of its single sound, alone and everywhere.

I know, now, that I am no longer like that.

4

I have changed remarkably.

It was not just those nights of shelling that did it. They were not unusually distressing, after all, especially after I began to notice that during those evenings everyone grew more affectionate, more gentle and careful. Sometimes I watched the nurses as they played cards. They eventually would find even the radio too annoying and would shut off its boring din, tired of listening to the news bulletins that came in such quick succession. They—both the nurses and the nuns—fed me bits of their delicious sandwiches, and they didn't even scold me for soiling my clothes, perhaps with a tomato slice that, coated with butter and mayonnaise, had slipped out from the white rounds of bread. We joked with each other. And we truly enjoyed ourselves once the others had been put to bed and had settled down. Those were the times when they would converse with me as if I were one of them, favoring me with their long and earnest stares.

"It's time you were let out of here," Sister St. Vincent-de-Paul would say as the others shook their heads sadly. I *had* gotten out once, after all. But then I had come back, after a period of time away that I could no longer reckon clearly.

Young, attractive Sister St. Vincent-de-Paul must be a close relative of Jesus Christ, I was sure. One day, with tears in her eyes, she had told me something of the life story of her patron saint, Vincent—or Mar Mansur, as we Lebanese call him. She must indeed be from the same family as Jesus Christ. I had the feeling that she knew him personally, as if they had sat together for a long while on the stone bench against the outer wall of a house overflowing with family members, some preparing food and others playing cards. Fixing their eyes on the distant horizon, surely they talked sweetly and sorrowfully about the wretched of the earth.

I was very fond of that nun. She did not have an exaggerated regard for rules, so I obeyed her every word. Sometimes she even left me alone when I was doing something that went against the rules, making it seem as though we shared some enduring secret. All of the others, though, were severe, as if they lived and worked for the sake of the hospital—for its buildings and its corridors—and not for the benefit of those inside. They liked the doctors much more than they liked us; they regarded us as victims of Satan's evil whisperings. All they wanted from us, especially on those nights of shelling, was that we stay huddled together—all of us, as silently as the dead—so that they could withdraw into their own fears, forgetting the anger of the Lord made incarnate in us. Forgetting the wrath that had been made visible through our transformation into creatures embodying divine retribution—creatures who then could be offered to believers as a visual sermon from which they must draw the most dreadful lessons.

But I was something different. And they knew that I had changed remarkably, for one day when I went (my face wet and my sobbing loud) to the Mother Superior and told her as I kissed her cross that I wanted to bathe alone, she gave me a very long look and then stared at the wall. "We will see," she told me.

In the beginning I despised the bathing. Although they took us into the bath only after our pills and tranquilizers had taken effect, my huge body never relaxed immediately or fully. Dragging me and four or five others into a large room, they stripped off the meager clothing we wore and sat us on the floor, with nothing between us and the wet tiles. They never paid any attention to the temperature of the water they spilled over us in such abundance that sometimes it arrested our breathing and jarred our heads practically into shock. The water might be freezing cold or burning hot, but it did not matter: they paid no attention to our protests. In next to no time we would relent, knowing it was useless to protest. Resignedly, we offered our rigid forearms to the rough, fibrous loofahs. I hated seeing myself naked—though it was even worse to see the others so—even if I knew that no one else was paying any attention to me. They flipped our bodies over, tugging us about in haste, unfeelingly, and causing pain to our thin, pallid bodies without even knowing or caring. They had no time to humor us, to coddle and care for us: there were many of us, but very little water. The tanker trucks transported it when there was plenty, but there also had to be fuel enough arriving to heat it. And we were full of complaints. All of us hated bath time, truly hated it. It frightened us to have that water poured over us.

It annoyed the nurses that they must handle us like children. Even if we were excessively gaunt, our adult bodies must have been heavy in their frail, flimsy state. And our only means of protest was to abandon our bodies to them, refusing to help them in any way. In the steam-filled air they perspired heavily above us as they did things that hurt our bodies—deliberately so, it seemed to us. But the pain we endured was one more thing that was alien to them. They had no experience of it—not them. They had no idea of what hurt us or of how we felt, no inkling of how we coped with the pain shooting through our bodies. So they teamed up against us, most of the time, provoking us because it distracted them and helped them to relax. They made jokes at our expense, jokes about us and our body parts, our private parts. It made them laugh. It made us laugh, too. We roared along with them as we stared at the targets of their teasing: it was as if those parts didn't belong to any of us. They made a great show of touching us there, as if those parts of ours had an importance that we could not possibly puzzle out. And most of the time our bath ended in general laughter, so much of it that we would refuse to get up, as we tried to devise ways to use up more time. We went to some length trying to bring their attention back to our sexual parts. But they were always in such a hurry. Giving us a scolding, they would pick us up and carry us out, wrapped in enormous white towels. They dressed us in clean white linen gowns, the sort that you close from the back with ties, and then they combed our hair before putting us back in bed to have our supper and go to sleep.

As for me, though: in the beginning they cared for me in a special way. They showed great tenderness toward my body. They handled it gently, and the nurse always kept me back after all of the others had left.

They were more careful and gentle with me at first because my body was unusually fragile for its size and the heavy thickness of my bones. My body still carried the traces of torture, although there were no longer so many marks, and those that were left were superficial. My wrist had been broken for too long—the hand dangling uselessly—to return now to its exact natural position. And for a while my back caused them trouble in the bath. They had to prevent the water from reaching my dressings. Whenever the loofah came within reach of a lingering bulge, they grew very gentle. Probing the area with their fingers, they repeated their questions without pausing for any responses from me. "What did those bastards do to you? What did those sons of bitches do? Just look at this body, this beautiful body, what it has become!"

But after a while they forgot all of it. Little by little, as my body slowly healed, erasing the marks of pain one by one, the nurses became irritated with me, especially as they began to see that I did not know what they were talking about and did not have any answers to their questions. They might not say so, but I could tell they were not even really certain that I felt any pain in those places.

Most of the time, then, our baths ended in laughter and joking. But there was one time when Nakhla went too far in his bath-time jesting with Jabir.

One of our nurses, Nakhla was generally crude and inconsiderate with us. Jabir is a Muslim, and so of course he is circumcised, which means that his sex does not look much like anyone else's. Maybe his circumcision made his sex look healthier than the thin and feeble privates the rest of us had. Whatever the reason, Nakhla kept at it, teasing Jabir relentlessly until finally another nurse came over and shoved Nakhla away. The pair of them went after each other right there in the bath, letting go with some fierce punches and slipping on the tile floor until the blood started coming. We were shocked and afraid, and we screamed until the supervisor came and managed to get them apart. He swore at them, reserving particular curses for Nakhla, and then they poured water over us hurriedly, dried us off with a roughness that seemed to communicate resentment, and took us out. They didn't comb our hair that day.

Later on, I did bathe alone, more or less whenever I wanted to or when there was enough water. And when Jabir returned—he had been out for a long time—we got to be friends. Of course, that did not happen right after he came back, but rather some time later.

We became such good friends that one day I said to him, "Jabir, tell my sister Asmaa, the next time she comes, tell her that you are me because I don't want to see her. . . ."

5

They believed I was mentally ill, and they showed how sorry they felt. Sorry because it was all a consequence, they agreed, of my kidnapping, of being held for a long time and tortured by my captors.

The young doctor, my sister Asmaa, the nuns, and the nurses believed it was all caused by my kidnapping and torture, as well as by my disappearance for such a long time in the capital city's western sector that everyone thought I had died. They brought me to Dayr al-Salib, the Convent of the Cross, after taking me out of the Cedar of Lebanon Hospital, where I had stayed—well, I can't remember now how long I stayed there. My sister Asmaa told me all of this as if it were another man's story, the story of someone whom I had never met. As far as she was concerned, I was completely insensible of everything that had happened to me.

Whenever Asmaa repeated the tale of what had happened to me—and she repeated it many times—she replaced one event with another and changed elements of the story. I would ask myself whether my sister was doing it deliberately. Perhaps it was a ploy to test my awareness and concentration. Would I discover her little game? Or perhaps she was altering the story, shortening here and adding there, for some purpose of her own. Or, I wondered, was she, too, suffering from distraction and forgetfulness? Or had she simply become more preoccupied with me, more worried than she had been before, and so was trying hard to make me understand that she loved me and wanted me to return to her, to the familiar territory she knew me as inhabiting once upon a time? I always listened to Asmaa in bewilderment, as if it really were the first time I had heard this narrative, which only served to confirm what was already fixed in her mind. She was absolutely convinced that I had been oblivious to everything that had happened to me. Even now, she was sure, I remained apart from it, distant . . . and so she would start in again, taking up her story.

I had known perfectly well that I was in the hospital—during the time when I really was a patient there, at Cedar of Lebanon—but then periodically I forgot all about it, especially when they pressed their insistent questions on me and then talked about me as if I were not there. They did not even seem aware of my presence as they offered reasons for my mental illness, which they went on attributing, vehemently and angrily, to my kidnapping and the torture sessions in the cellars of West Beirut.

I had been coming down off the heights that morning, singing all the while I was sneaking horizontally along the mountainside. The sun was about to come up. Some youths who, like me, were cutting through the rough mountain terrain stopped me. I did not see them until they were very close, for in their camouflage uniforms they blended in finely with the rocks and scrub.

When they noticed traces of blood on my shirt, they surrounded me. Inching closer, they aimed their rifles at my chest. They stripped off my clothes and made me kneel on the ground, my hands clasped over my head. Though the scene depressed me slightly, I did not feel greatly affected. They had nothing to do with me, I decided, and I would not speak to them. They searched and searched through my clothes. When they found no papers to establish my identity, they began talking among themselves as if I were not there. Good, I said to myself. For a few moments they were silent and still, and then they suddenly swarmed over me and started to beat me and question me. I was thinking, miserably, what a wretched coincidence it was that I had encountered these particular people at a moment of such enormous joy, the very moment in which I had regained my soul and taken hold of it, fresh, pure, and whole, my newborn spirit. It had happened precisely in that moment when I no longer had any bond to the things of this world, the moment in which I floated above the mundane and watched it retreat in haste, fleeing downward from my feet and my song. Now, as they hit me, I repeated a single phrase. *Ya Allah.* O God. *Ya Allah.*

They went on beating me for a long time. But it was then, in a single flash of perception, that I experienced a stunning realization. I had not lost that happiness of mine, I saw; I had not lost it in the least. All in a flash that recognition came, and I knew as I watched the blood spurt from my mouth and all over my naked body that the ache I felt was not pain. It was nothing at all like any pain I had known before, all of those times when despite my strength I would scream in agony and anger if I so much as struck my knee carelessly against a jutting corner. I began to contemplate this new pain as if it were all a dream. This was me, in pain; but it wasn't me. It was my body in pain; but it was not my body. It felt as though I were a mere spectator. And it felt as though I had two bodies. Not like the two bodies I used to have, bodies that kept me in agony when they split and drew apart and then again as they came together. Two bodies, but two *other* bodies. Different ones.

These young men were striking me hard. And I was watching it all, unable to believe what I was seeing. As they kept on hitting me, I fell, staring at the pebbles that grew larger and larger to fill my field of vision. I could hear myself sucking in the flying specks of dirt that had stuck to the blood coming out of my nose. And it still seemed as if I were just watching, an onlooker following every movement precisely for no other reason than a compelling desire to know everything. With every slap a shudder coursed through my whole body, but the pain lingered only at the point where the blow had landed. It did not reach as far as my head or come even close to touching my heart. When I realized as much, I began to laugh. They bound my hands and feet and carried me off to somewhere far away.

When I awoke, I found that they had roped my middle with a thin but strong cord that they had drawn very tight. I had been thrown on the floor and left alone in a darkened place. I knew that I was swelling fast and that bruises must be erupting across my body. Now and then they came to me. They would sit down near me and try gently and quietly to get me to talk so that I could relieve myself of my secret—so they said—and extricate myself from this situation. Sometimes they stared at me, bewildered, and I would hear one of them murmur that I really was crazy, that I wasn't faking it after all. But then someone else would answer testily: I was a dangerous man and a liar; I had killed someone, and they needed to know my story. At still other times they concluded that I must be killed so that they would be rid of my odor. But then it wasn't long before they would go back to hitting me and asking their questions. "Talk . . . Talk!" And me—my head was blank. There was nothing inside but the longing to go back to my song, the one I had been absorbed in setting to music . . . coming down across the mountainside in that lovely dawn. . . .

"Talk."

"What should I say? What, brothers?"

They would be furious. Either that or they were afraid of me. They pounded at me. I stared hard to see where the blows would hit, but in the darkness I could make out very little.

In my many spells of amnesia I did not know how or when they moved me to a dark room where I found myself held with other people. There I improved in that the aches in my body lessened, but I did have diarrhea frequently. I slept much of the time, waking sometimes to find that my companions had changed, that the faces I saw were not the ones I had left when I went to sleep.

One day they came in carrying some nice-looking navy blue tracksuits with white stripes. It made me happy to see with them the young man from the militia who liked me, I think, because he was always joking with me. This young fellow spoiled me, bringing me decent chocolate bars once in a while, giving me pills to stop the diarrhea, and talking to me. I know that sometimes he laughed at me and made fun of my appearance to his comrades, but I sensed that he really did like me, and so I would tell myself that he was just going along with them. When he was there, I felt a measure of contentment. Whenever he was late, I would start missing him.

They washed me that day without any grumbling or the usual shouting and slapping. They dressed me in a tracksuit. They said to us, "We are going to return you to your people. It's a hostage-exchange operation, so everyone get ready." A man next to me was so happy he burst out crying and thanking his Lord, sobbing the words out loud. I searched through my head for a long time, asking myself what it meant that they were going to "return us to our people," until I located Asmaa somewhere in my brain. I realized that they would return me to Asmaa.

All of us were happy except for one person. As I stared at him, wondering, I recalled that he had been with me in this place for a long time. Then I remembered that he was the university professor. I knew this because he had said it so often—that he was a university professor and had nothing to do with any of this. That had all been before he fell into a permanent silence, like me—or almost like me. Now he was the only one among us who seemed afraid and nervous. And when the others asked him why, he said, "You stupid people, they're going to kill us. They will take us out of here and kill us." The man who had been thanking his Lord out loud wailed at him, "Why are you saying that? Would they have brought us tracksuits if they were going to kill us?"

A long time passed as we waited in our tracksuits. Gradually I slipped into oblivion.

6

It was nighttime when I awoke to the realization that we were in a bus. It swung sharply with us as it zigzagged rapidly along a dilapidated road in the darkness, moving between huge wild bushes that slapped hard against the glass of the windows. I heard the howling of dogs, lots of them, running alongside us and barking. Out of the cavernous blackness they would appear suddenly and momentarily: craning their necks on the other side of the glass, opening their huge jaws, then freezing in place, and barking on and on.

The bus came to a stop, and the headlights went out. Our guards climbed down, except for one who stayed behind to watch us. No one made a sound. I was afraid—me and the university professor, who was very pale and shook violently in his seat.

After we had waited a short time, a man from the Red Cross climbed into the bus, accompanied by a young, light-haired foreigner. They began speaking in English and shaking their heads mournfully as they examined us at close range.

They shepherded us off the bus and lined us up, our backs pressed against the metallic side of our vehicle. I wanted to stretch my legs, but when I started to walk, our guard reprimanded me, so I returned to my place in the lineup. The silence was heavy and so absolute that I could hear the professor's pee trickling down onto the dirt through his pant legs.

"That guy over there just peed in his clothes and got his clean suit dirty," I said to them. The man from the Red Cross came over to me.

"Calm down, everything is all right."

"The fellow is crazy," said the professor. "Gag him, tie him up—he's going to get all of us killed." His jaw was trembling so hard he could hardly get the barely audible words out of his mouth.

"Calm down," the man from the Red Cross said to him. "Everything will be all right."

I began to shake my head in sympathy. Laughter was welling up inside my chest, though, little chuckles that shook my body and that I found difficult to control. The professor kept saying, "I kiss your feet, have mercy on us. I kiss your hands, show us some kindness."

Then he went silent, and I assumed a waiting pose, quiet and deferential like the others. The Red Cross man came over to me and examined my hand and forearm, still bound up in a clean strip of cloth. I would not let him touch me. He stepped away, and I began to look around, but in the thick darkness I could not make out anything.

Across from us there seemed to be another group of people who were waiting just as we were. I began to ask myself how the exchange would be handled. There would be a broad plaza, I imagined, well lit and exposed so that it would be easily visible. In the middle of this open square, so like a large playing field, there of course would stand a dignified, solemn man. He must appear distinguished so that everyone on both sides would put their trust in him. This man would be holding something—a flag, for instance—that he would lift high as he recited one name from over here and one from over there. Those whose names were called would step forward from the darkness into the light, walking cautiously but steadily until they reached the spot where he stood. He would say something to them—what it would be I didn't know—and they would shake hands. The handshaking was an essential part of it, I thought. At that point the man would blow the whistle that hung down his chest as he waved the flag in his hand. In that exact instant the two men who were to be exchanged would scurry off, each heading away from the place where he had emerged into the light. Each one would arrive at his destination at exactly the same moment, returning to his people, and everyone would hug everyone else. And so it would go until all the kidnap victims had been exchanged. Then I told myself that the dignified man would be from the Red Cross. He would have to be. Perhaps even from the International Red Cross—that is, the foreign one, not our local one. That would provide more credibility and objectivity so that no one would doubt his impartiality. When I tried to form an image of this man, I found that I was picturing him in sports clothes that would go well with our tracksuits, though perhaps with a few details that would set him apart. I started to laugh.

But when they snapped at me, I got quiet and went back to my silent musing. I began to sink into a gloom. I realized that the hostage-exchange scene I had sketched out in my mind had no space in it for me. With this body of mine I would not be able to run like the people in my scene had done. And my sister Asmaa would be disturbed and upset. It's just like it always is, she would tell herself. There he is again, lagging behind his companions, exactly as he always has. Wherever he is, he's always behind everyone else—and then he falls down before he can reach the finish line.

I heard shots.

"Oh my God! Mama!" we all began to scream. The Red Cross man yanked at my collar and pulled me down to the ground. He dragged me behind him until we were beneath the bus, wedged between the tires. The shells went on exploding as we all pressed ourselves together, the foreign man saying, "Oh shit, oh shit, it can't be, oh God."

When it stopped, they led us back into the bus. The hostage-exchange operation had failed, they said.

That was what they told us through their microphones after the bus came to a stop. When the Red Cross men had gone, our guards got us out of the bus with blows and kicks. They pushed us into a room. It was a new one, not the one we had been in before, and we were crowded in there.

But when they wanted to take back the tracksuit, I lost control. "This doesn't belong to you," I snapped at them. "It is from the Red Cross. I won't give it back." I returned their slaps, blow for blow, and finally they left me alone with the tracksuit. They went out, shutting the doors and windows behind them as they swore at us.

The university professor was crying. "I knew it," he sobbed. "Now they will kill us because our group doesn't have any hostages left. They lined them up and shot them. All of them. I know it. We're in for it." His voice was so full of emotion that we believed him. Some of the other men started to cry. "Yes, they'll kill us now, you're right," they agreed.

But they did not kill us. I don't have any recollection now of how the prisoner exchange went forward or of how they exchanged me. I do not remember who was with me or when it all took place or what time it was when they went ahead, though the operation was obviously crowned with success. I can't remember anything about it at all because the amnesia comes so often.

They got me to understand that I was in Cedar of Lebanon Hospital and told me what had happened. They had returned me to my family after I'd been kidnapped and tortured and exchanged, they told me. From that day on, Asmaa repeated her versions of it to me, over and over. Every time it was a new story she told, and she seemed convinced that I was completely unconscious of everything that had happened or was happening to me. Everyone agreed that my forgetfulness and then my mental illness were because of my kidnapping and torture. And Asmaa went on telling me the story, which was yet another new story. . . .

7

It makes no sense for plants not to lean toward the sunlight. It makes no sense for plants to have an aversion to the sun.

I pace to the window and back, drawn to what is in front of it as much as to what lies beyond it, to the circle of light falling onto the white tiles and the space that the others leave to me because they do not like the light. Before, I was just like them. I suffered as they did from the overpowering whiteness that the walls and floor send back amplified. Walls and floor magnify the whiteness; they do not reflect it back to us muted and quiet; they do not absorb any of those stinging needles that pierce your head through to the back of your skull. They reflect it as a hard shine, a sharp brightness. The floor tiles and the walls, glossy with paint that washes easily, transformed each head into a burning point of light, bouncing to us from the thousands of turning, shivering mobile mirrors surrounding us.

We were hunted by the light, tracked by the whiteness, encircled like wild animals in traps. We could not find a remedy: it made no difference to close our eyes, nor did it help to poke our heads into the corners or under the bed covers. Even late into the night we were exposed to the violence and harm of the light because they left the lights on. And when the electricity was cut off, they hung huge gas-powered lamps over our heads or those tiny ones that look like specks, fed by batteries and eternally lit. We could not shade our eyes from them. How could they not have seen that the light was a source of permanent pain for us, loading and tensing our nerves all the way to the tiniest, remotest filaments that lay slack like tubes left open, vulnerable to a raging current that is unstoppable? It was one long, unending, electrifying sting; and we would press ourselves into the corners, contracting our eyes and limbs as much as we could, to evade the touch of those surfaces as we fell like bloated, indigestible snails. But then the light would draw us back to the exposed center of the room.

That light hurt so much that we had to give in to it. So much that the pupils of our eyes would begin their peculiar rolling, every which way in a desperate search for the dark interior somewhere within the eyeball. Only our eyes maintained the frantic quest for an escape from the light and the whiteness, even from their own whiteness.

The iris would fester, and our eyelids would jump nervously in their tiny margin; and whether or not curtained by the eyelid's moist and salty film, the pupil went on circling, tensing toward the inside of the head, toward the feeble, tepid darkness there, leaving to the exterior light the whites of the eyes that alone can accustom themselves to that greater whiteness.

Everything was white, brightly lit, unbearably bright. Walls, floor tiles, beds, bed linens, tables, window shutters, windowpanes, grilles over the windowpanes, window frames, doctors, nurses, nuns, the wings on the nuns' headdresses that fluttered slowly on the cottony white breeze as they passed by, the nuns' shoes. Very rarely, and only when the heat was intense, did we catch tiny glimpses of the nuns' bare feet, the shape of their toes, which we committed to memory: all the curves and angles, the dry cracks in elderly feet and then the softness—the pretty regularity and freshness—of the feet of Sister St. Vincent-de-Paul, the saint who was beautiful all the way to her toes.

On winter days we got a small respite as the sky bent low and darkened and the fine needles retreated from our heads. When it rained, we felt so happy, hearing that lovely, out-of-doors sound that wrapped round the buildings and enveloped the entire hill. We listened with such concentration to its gentle clatter on the roofs, its rustling on the leaves of trees and plants, and its tat-a-tat over the glistening surfaces of the open walkways.

Surely the rain brought back our memories, sounds we had known in a faraway past, and although we could not exactly trace the sounds to their actual sources, they carried us off to another point, somewhere other than the place we were in. The sounds of the rain bore us away to locations and moments of childhood. Under a balcony roof on the way to some school, our leather book bags held over our heads. Or huddled next to a heating stove among people who knew us well, people whom we were accustomed to see, the talk around us becoming a sweet cacophony of voices raining down on our skin like lovely quilts beneath which we could doze off. When it rained, we grew calm, for that delicious patter transported us to places we knew even without identifying them precisely. We would take in familiar smells, reminiscent of the waters of the warm bath steaming gently over the odor of the kerosene from the water heater, which would set up a pleasant rattle in front of the door to the bathroom, whose lone window, looking out on level ground, we covered with our dirty clothes before our mothers poured hot water across the floor to keep our feet from shivering on the cold tiles. Or, at the sound of the rain, we were once again standing at the doors to warm ovens, passing the hot loaves from hand to hand as we looked up at the sky, afraid to get the inviting bread wet, stealing bites, uncertain how to get it home before its split halves stuck together and its wondrous steam vanished.

We would get quiet when the rain clattered on the roofs because we were hearing it on other roofs, on a Sunday afternoon among our cousins, shaking with laughter that we tried to suppress as we hid under a huge wool blanket in the darkness of our collective breathing.

Hearing the *khashkhasha* of the rain, we suddenly would be standing in faraway places. Standing there for a quickly passing, transitory moment perhaps, but always in a childhood there and gone, so that we were left only with a swift and sudden surprise, the remote taste of that childhood lingering briefly in our throats, a tang that returned effortlessly but would not stay. A taste that came back with ease and then disappeared rapidly, leaving us astonished, bewildered by the immense adult bodies here before us—yes, bewildered, as if these bodies had appeared all of a sudden and we had no idea of their function or how to use them. These were bodies we weren't accustomed to, bodies that wouldn't obey us. They slipped away from us, and so we would forget about them; but then we would have to face them again, discovering that they had aged even more, become more distant and even stranger than before. And as weak and submissive as they were, they would become yet more difficult to master and tame, to adopt as our own. We fled from these bodies because we could see how remote they were from what they had been on those days when, in a faraway childhood, we had listened to the rustling of the rain on the trees, its clatter on the rooftops and the glistening pavements.

Now I stand next to the window because I am no longer like them. I stand here because I need to keep my distance from them. I want to forget them, to forget how much like them I am. To forget how my body is entangled in theirs, how my body loses itself among their bodies, loses itself in their multitude, their fear of the whiteness, their meek submission to whatever they face. In their self-abnegation, they offer themselves before the anger of the Lord like a flock on whom He has lowered the knife of retribution, on whom He has visited His choice of flawed and faulty forms. Like a flock of lost sheep they are, a cluster that He has selected, unhurriedly, waving them aside: these are the bad sheep whom He has made no effort to return to His blessed flock cavorting on the outside, grazing in the bounty and grace He has bestowed, pastured in forgiveness and the erasure of sins, in the blessed forgetfulness of that grace and its mercy.

Those on the outside—they were the innocents who always do what the Lord commands of them, who obey Him in times of peace as in the civil wars. He did not tire of them, nor did He declare Himself as our portion, as the blessed lot of the lost sheep that we were. He was not ours, not the Hope we could entreat. We were the reckoning that He forsook in hopelessness, incensed at the sickly yellowness of that retributive justice—at our frail, paralytic organs, at the delirium and the ulcerous sores, at the way we banged our heads against the wall and howled in the night like despised wild dogs whose cries break savagely into sweet evenings of warmth and passion. The ones outside, the blessed ewes, they have always been more entertaining, more enjoyable and diverting than we can ever be. More lively, more voluble, more changeable. So the Lord changed his mind and his camp; the Lord sat down with them, sat among them like a father. And He left us. He abandoned us to our bodies and to that bright, incandescent whiteness that He hath brought down upon us in His rage and His fury.

And so when I did leave this place, it was not long before I returned.

And then I knew that the Lord had not let me go.

8

I stand at the window. I stand here for what is before it and for what lies beyond it.

It is the light that tugs my limbs, that draws them toward heat and purity, toward the point where I can follow the dust prancing across the ground into the ray of light that splatters there, where I set down my bare feet to warm them, to study them for hours at a time. To play with my toes, toying with the nails and kneading the white skin calcified around and over them. To know that this space is mine alone, and as I rest here to feel certain that I am no longer like the others, the ones who remain inside, huddled in the corners of their room or on their beds, or underneath them.

When I hear the tinkle of the rain, I draw myself up and look. I stand at the window and lean my head against the metal grille that protects us from splintering or exploding glass. It is the glass that lets me see things without blending into them. I gaze down over the garden that the white metal grille cuts up into big squares, like the ones I used to trace when I needed to draw an accurate geographical map, keeping the distances between points correct and to scale. I divide the garden into squares that I examine one by one until a flock of delicate birds bursting from the wet trees attracts my gaze and I follow their flight with my eyes . . . until my eyes move abruptly off of a single square to fix on the whole space: that's what happens, sometimes, when I see her.

I see her sitting in the garden. She sits on the ground beneath a brilliant sun. Just sits, motionless, doing nothing. I forget that she is dead. I forget outright. Or perhaps I don't know that she is dead. I go on looking at her and waiting. I wait until she turns toward me, until she becomes aware that I am here or until she says something. I wait until she moves so that I can see what she will do. Then I forget that she is in front of me and that I'm watching her from the window. Perhaps I remember again, and she is there in my line of sight, in exactly the same pose as before, wholly still. And then I get annoyed. I step away from the window, telling myself that all I'm seeing is a picture. A picture that is not real. When I go back to the window, I don't see her there. I just see the white squares and the rain. Or I do see her—under the bright sun, still there, still unmoving. Perhaps, then, I feel sad, but not very and not for long. If I feel happy, it's a sensation that soon vanishes. It doesn't bother me to see that woman in the garden, on the other side of the window, any more than it pleases or cheers me to see her after so much time has passed. I just become confused and uncomfortable. I'm confused about where to place that woman inside of me, when she is there, just like that, motionless in front of the window. Where to put her, inside of me, where to make a place just for her? Does she belong inside the happiness or inside the sadness? Inside what I can remember or inside what I have forgotten? Does she go with the longing or with the irritation? With the yearning or with the boredom of repetition? Her repetition, hers, the repeating of her inside of me.

When she sat there for a long time outside without moving, most often I cried. Cried and cried, on and on, and out loud. I could never understand whether I cried from pain and anger or from overpowering happiness.

Part Two

1

I saw her at the shop of a relative of mine. He sold produce, and his shop faced the village square.

I felt a pounding in my chest. "Can't be," I said. "It's just a woman who looks like her."

I was on the opposite pavement, some distance from her. I stepped back, shielding myself in the crowd of passersby, repeating, "It's just a woman who looks like her." I walked a few steps forward cautiously, fearful that she might see me, but she seemed completely engrossed in her own affairs. I got quite near, after making sure that the car between us would conceal me from her even if she turned around to take in the scene.

She was wholly occupied in filling several sacks with vegetables and fruit. She smiled at the other women who were picking through the same carton and exchanged brief words with them. She looked at her hands, noticed the dirt, and wiped them on a paper bag. She chatted lightly with my relative, the produce vendor. She bargained with him, but not for very long, and she paid him. He carried her bags to the trunk of a small car. She got in and put on a pair of sunglasses. She glanced around before driving off through the crowds in the souk, disappearing from sight.

I did not ask my relative, the produce seller, about her. He would have answered me with a flood of questions. If I were to say that she had been a classmate of mine at the university, he would mention me to her—just to have something to say. He would remark to her, "Did you know . . . your friend from university, he's from my family, you know, so-and-so." And he would point me out to her as soon as he saw me anywhere close to his shop. Or else he would notice that I was watching her but never coming up to speak to her.

I did not ask my relative, the grocer, about her because it was clear to me that she was a frequent customer at his shop. I was also not at all certain that I wanted to speak to her or to see her again.

Over the next two days she came and went constantly inside my head. I would catch myself smiling stupidly at nothing, easily distracted and inattentive, going about in a state of cheerful inactivity, unable to make up my mind about anything. When Asmaa asked me if I wanted coffee, I had to ponder her question before I could answer. I gave serious thought to whether I really wanted coffee before resuming my conversation with visitors whose presence, wreathed in smiles beneath the trellis outside our house, had abruptly come to my attention. I made sincere efforts to enter into a conversation whose ends our visitors gathered under the trellis on the veranda, a conversation that would come and go, but always in the same region, between our legs and over our heads, under the trellis—come and go and reach in all directions, returning me to the profound sense that had clung to me since childhood of being a character out of an ancient story. I was not really there among them then to pick up and hold the strand of conversation that was mine to grasp, the end of it held out toward me. And when I was there among them, I was not really among them, but rather alone, gazing hard at what they did not look at. What I mean is, I was gazing hard at them. Holding them in my stare, I could not stop asking myself why they had come. Why do the visitors come? I was not convinced that visiting lessened anyone's tedium. I had always liked seeing visitors at our house, but I did not like to participate in the conversation. As a child, I could come in and out, weaving my way among the visitors, and no one paid any attention to me. Their presence delighted me because it meant that no one was watching, so I could do as I pleased. When visitors were present,

I found our house more attractive and orderly, and my family seemed more affectionate and pleasant, more easy-going, more refined. Among the crowd sat little tables bearing plates of appealing fruit, demitasses of coffee, and colorful packs of cigarettes. Pastries or bonbons or roasted seeds sat on starched tablecloths that we removed from the tables as soon as the visitors had gone. It was one minor holiday or another, and I didn't care what it was as long as there were delicacies left over for me to taste at my leisure, good things in paper napkins that I could proudly give my friends to try. But I grew older, and it came time for me to sit with the visitors whether I wanted to do so or not. I was older, and now there was a strand of the conversation meant for me to seize. An end, a part, for me, that no one would take on my behalf or indulgently let me neglect.

And so, over the next two days, she came and went ceaselessly inside my head. I began to explain it to myself as the effect of my restless idleness, for that woman had never been important in my life. In our last couple of encounters I didn't treat her with much seriousness; I probably sounded as if I were mocking her. I felt myself eagerly shrugging off a burden that there'd been no good reason to shoulder. I began thinking that she really wasn't even very pretty and didn't deserve even the amount of effort a minor and short-lived adventure required. Nor did she have the sort of quick cleverness that would afford me the pleasure of playing the game and planning my maneuvers. She didn't stimulate my appetite strongly enough to induce me to endure her coarse and unpolished habits, her clingy ways, and her simpleminded, out-of-proportion reactions. I couldn't stand her use of grand words and the eloquent rhetoric of the self-styled intellectual who fancies herself at a crucial and sensitive stage that will long be remembered and invoked, one that demands a well-thought-out verbal design that will appear original and powerful.

I half listened to her string of words, I recalled, as I gazed at her and assumed an expression of melancholy or of sympathetic thoughtfulness or of a combination of the two sometimes. I was so certain of never seeing her again that instead of making my delight obvious, I began imploring her—yes, practically begging her—not to leave me. I set about explaining, intimating that I was so smitten that it was causing me agonies of pain, but I was submitting to fate in the shape of her pronouncements because everything in life called me to utter despair. What propelled me to play this game—to lie to her—was the irritation and fatigue that her continued presence left in me, plus a touch of scorn for this creature whose mind and presence seemed bent on sketching a portrait of grandiose and awkward self-importance. This woman . . . I reminded myself that never again would this wretched woman be given such an opportunity to bask in her sense of self-importance. I was granting her this chance not out of compassion for her, but because I knew that she did not begin to merit hearing my inner feelings, finding out what was truly passing through my mind. She would not understand it at all, anyway. Her petty mind, its boundaries as unmistakable as the rectangular lines of a box of matches, would merely tell her that I was envious, that was all, and that my masculine sense of honor and dignity refused to accept that a woman would leave me. Had I really been besotted with her, the whole thing would have been a drama indeed. That is what I told myself again and again as she, facing me, gurgled tears that she swallowed ostentatiously. Oh my God, I was telling myself, what a poor wretch I would have become had I really been infatuated with this miserable woman.

Meanwhile, she was designing the layout of her words with great care, fully aware that they were meant to be long remembered. Meant for posterity. She was imagining the scene, seeing herself, and seeing me as an old man as I summoned the moment back in my memory, all the while sighing my eternal regret and declaring repeatedly that she was the woman I had never been able to forget, the only one among all women. As I looked at her, the thought came to me that all women conduct themselves as if they're in a film. They always catapult themselves into its most climactic slice, a moment that is eternal, that lasts until old age, until my old age to be exact. The dotage of the hero. . . . She was laying her words out carefully, pausing to leave spaces of silence so her words would imprint themselves on my memory. She selected her words with that other woman—the heroine—in mind. All the moments of farewell reflect that sole moment and always return to it. One moment of farewell, universally applicable, shared by all, a moment that hardly changes from one film to the next, for we collapse all the moments into one image, putting them all on one level no matter how widely scattered and differentiated they are. We see ourselves on an enormous screen, floodlit by the sadnesses we will carry. Our voices issue from that immense space that confronts us head on, emerging from the vast time of memory to come. We hear our sad voices coming to us from within the grief and regret that will inevitably be our lot. We hear them as corrupted, "off," transformed, and altered as they come to us from endless tapes, narrow streams of recorded sound, concentrated, crisscrossing, before they spread as sound waves, then scatter. It is the unique moment of farewell, one in which we see double. We see ourselves as we are in the present, but we also see ourselves overlain by our grief to come. We see compassion, always accompanied by steadfast courage, eternal stoicism: the philosophy of Zeno the Stoic. With Zeno we stroll the stoa: we walk along his porch that hears our footfalls and witnesses our intrepid composure as we draw near to its farther end. She and I and Zeno; and with us are all the heroes from the one and only film of farewell, and with us too is passion, giving out its death rattle.

All of this went through my mind as I sat there before her. I shook my head in regret and sadness and understanding and asked myself how I could make her hear out loud what I was thinking. She was hanging her pretty little head like a ship mast broken by violent waves brought on by a storm. Violent waves in a glass of water. A tempest in a teacup. Could be the water glass on the table between us.

I knew perfectly well that she was lying—and perhaps, in the end, that was why I felt as I did. All instances of farewell, like this one, are deceptions, for they always involve one of two possibilities. The first is that she no longer loves me or never did; or, she loved me, but then ceased loving me for some reason—perhaps for no reason at all. In this case the moment of parting, or the farewell, is based on two components, two people. One of those two parties wants to be rid of the other but makes the assumption, of course, that this other person is so full of feeling that he does not even sense that the first party has stopped loving him, so it is necessary to make him understand this by using very clear and unequivocal terms. And since I was that other party who (it is supposed) must be actively gotten rid of, I would endeavor to play my role with the least possible fuss and so as to abbreviate the necessary formalities. I assumed the expression of a saddened lover, miserable but resigned, so that she would preserve a good image of me, a sweet and disinterested trace, but one quick to fade so that she would not succeed in inscribing the parting as the eternally resonant and dramatic moment of her imaginings. . . .

The second possibility was that she loved me but needed the rites of a formal parting to lend more significance to her emotions, to get my attention, to let me know that I wasn't loving her enough, to threaten me that she was about to leave, to make me taste the sadness that I would doubtless have to endure, in pain, if she were indeed to leave me. This second sort of farewell is just as deceptive as the first because it is for the purpose of retaining, not losing. It means union, not severance; it means more of everything, a stronger tie, greater togetherness. In it, one says to the other partner: hold on to me more tightly, and do not leave me. Know that my presence cannot be taken for granted. Remember that I am not you. I am another person, and I just might detach my being from yours, leaving you severed. Leaving you in loss. This farewell says: love me more. Prevent me from going. Erase this possibility.

All moments of farewell are lies, for they fall into one of these two possibilities. Those who truly want a parting of ways, who want to cut the tie, do not come together and talk. They do not offer excuses; they leave no empty spaces between their perfectly crafted sentences. They try to forget and to relinquish, not to produce endless symbolic legacies and everlasting monuments.

I gaze at her—observing herself and me and that eternal moment that she finds us to be in—and I know that I will not demand her back. Hardly likely, I muse, that this is an instance of the first alternative; I doubt that she's out of love with me and wants only to rid herself of me so that she can go off to someone else. The second possibility seems more likely: that is, the farewell gesture as an invitation to more passion, a gesture that will lead me to hold on to her all the more tightly. In either case, she's triggering my irritation, she's whipping up a truly cosmic antagonism. And naturally I will not try to get her back. I will disappear for a while, acting like a guy who wants to be alone with his sorrows and wholly devoted to them, someone who renounces earthly life and withdraws from society. Then, somewhat later, I'll show myself; I'll make sure that she sees me, but I'll make no effort to get her back. I'll let her observe me in a state of melancholy induced by my passion, but looking completely resigned to the decision she's made to say good-bye and leave me. I'll look convinced that the subject is closed, the matter now reduced to preserving those precious memories. She'll recognize that I will never try in the slightest to conciliate her or to contrive means and invent pretexts to regain the time that has been lost. I will look sad but cold, empty of the longing that she is so accustomed to seeing in me, whose reappearance she must have been hazarding. Then, after a time, I will arrange things so that she sees me with other women. I will help her to believe that I am struggling to find solace and distracting myself with the foolish superficialities of other females now that I have been renounced and rejected by Woman in Her Essence: barred from the Woman she is. Then, little by little, I will bring myself to find a morsel of enjoyment in those discarded husks of life. I will take only a little pleasure in my state, but I will find some enjoyment in it. I will try to give her—gradually but definitively—the place she has chosen. I will laboriously place her, forever, in the charming frame she has drawn with her own artistic fingers. I will make her see that my attempts have succeeded—that I have set her into that film of eternal meaning.

These thoughts were all going through my mind. But I was also considering how I might get away quickly without breaking the rhythm, so I did not really take in her well-wrought sentences. The care she took with her phrasing seemed rather insolent to me, as if the logic she set out were stronger than I. In fact, she was sounding logical, or at least her sentences appeared so. By means of that logic she was fortifying herself against me, as if I were not even there in front of her, as if I were not at that moment looking into her eyes. That logic kept her strong, as if my body were not there with all of its compelling equipment. My body, there on the other side of the table.

I wasn't hearing her words. I just wanted badly to go away, but I stayed still, and I stayed calm. Studying my own composure, I decided it was agreeable, and I told myself that I would try to appear even more tranquil, for there was nothing here to justify impatience. Whenever I became aware that she awaited some sort of answer or comment from me, I gave her a weak smile and shook my head forlornly, saying whatever came to me that would tell her I was in a bad way, a very bad way. At one point the idea came to me of laughing and clapping her on the shoulder to make her laugh with me about what we had gotten ourselves into so intensely—how we'd brought ourselves to the very edge, conjured up a serious and hazardous state of affairs that appeared inevitable, inescapably imposed on us. I considered saying to her: C'mon, girl, let's move on! We're not entertaining ourselves as we should be, and we're not giving any thought to time that's wasting. We are true feather-brains if we can convince ourselves that we are weighty factors in the shaping of a true and momentous History, that we are nothing less than torrential tributaries emptying fiercely, moment by moment, into the eternal and everlasting river of human experience as it pours forth to pierce Time itself. It's all just a silly little lie, you know. Why, I'm barely able to keep myself convinced that I'm really here. . . .

I thought of laughing with all my heart, of kissing her on the cheek and pulling her hard by the hand and shouting, "Go on, now, and may God protect you! No one owes anyone anything, and it's as simple as that, and you've nothing to lose sleep over." But she was so strongly convinced by her own performance, by our performance. And since she was saying good-bye to me, she was the one who had to choose the perfect, eloquent moment that would seal our farewell. She had to conduct her own exit. So she gathered together her belongings that lay on the table and declared, her voice faint, that she could not be any later than she already was. I stood up, silent, and offered to accompany her to her home. She refused my gallantry, of course, saying there was nothing to justify my making the effort because conditions were clear and the atmosphere was completely calm. And her home was a goodly distance away. That's true, I told myself; her home really is a long way from here. It had been a lot of trouble to take her home at night—or, later, to take her to the border, which was as far as I could go on the route to her faraway home when it became even farther away, and then farther still.

She left, her steps slow so that I would not think she was in such a hurry to be rid of me. Or perhaps she hoped I would stop her. I would take her hand (which hung empty and idle), and I would pull her back to me, enveloping her in a forceful embrace as I exclaimed how ridiculous it all was, told her I would see her tomorrow, and laughed. And then she would laugh, her eyes still full of tears, her face next to mine. Or I would take her by the hand to a taxi, and we'd go to Samaan's house, where I would sleep with her, and all resolutions to separate would be forgotten. Perhaps that is what she wanted. But I didn't do any of these things because I felt no desire for her. The only desire I had was to stop seeing her in front of me and hearing her voice in my ears.

"I won't see you again, then?" I asked her, my tone calibrated to the dramatic requirements of the situation. "Yes, of course you will," she said. "Of course we will meet; after all, we are friends." We are friends. Of course we are. After all, how could we possibly go our separate ways unless she wrapped up the scene with expressions that were more suitable? Or at least with words more indicative of the limits and capacities of this small and superficial creature that lived inside her pretty head, a head attached and bound and operated by strips of film. Oh my God!

We are friends. After I left her, I started to say it over and over in my head—we are friends, we are friends—out of self-mockery, or just because I was feeling irritated at her and at the whole situation. I looked at my watch and decided I would go over to see Lamyaa of the big breasts. After all, Lamyaa and I are friends, too. Indeed, we are real friends. "Lamyaa," I'll say to her, "Lamyaa, we are friends. And I wasted a lot of time by staying away from your big breasts. Even though I never really abandoned them."

Then I asked myself what the point was. What do I have to do with women, anyway? I'll go home and get some sleep. But I wasn't sleepy, and the idea came to me of putting together something that evening where I could see my buddies, and we could enjoy ourselves and drink the night away. I altered my route toward Samaan's house, which was nearby. But I found him alone, and the electricity was cut off, as was the phone line. So we couldn't contact anyone. I didn't stay with him long because the heavy, depressed atmosphere of his home was completely unsuitable to my carefree, febrile state of mind.

As I headed home, though, my irritation returned. How, I asked myself, how could I have allowed so much time to elapse without really taking account of this creature's insipid spirit and limited mind? I recalled, too, that it was she who had chosen, for this final rendezvous, to sit in a café where the walls are decorated with tourist posters showing Baalbek and the vast Cedars of Lebanon, outlined in little seashells. It all seemed an uncomfortable blow to my self-pride. And I had to admit, unhappily, that if she had truly been taken with me, she would have chosen a place of more warmth and intimacy. She would have found a place less public and less repellent than that hideous spot, which surely a woman should have found difficult to select as a venue in which to tell her beloved good-bye. Women do take great interest in settings, in the atmosphere that a place intimates. In any case, I told myself, I'm rid of her.

Some days later I remembered the vow I had made to myself: I would bring about a scenario where she would catch sight of me at a distance. She would not be able to avoid seeing me; what's more, she would see that I was not trying to cling to her or to restore a moment that was gone forever. But when I set about putting my stratagem into practice, I discovered that she had already gotten to the second stage of my plan on her own. I saw her heading toward a car in which a classy-looking young man waited. She was the one, I realized then, who was reaching for life's husks in her efforts to forget me. But the difference was that she had no idea that I was on hand and watching. It was not her intent to make me see her. That made all the difference.

But I didn't feel humiliated, nor did I feel any anger or a sense of betrayal. I very nearly laughed. When I tried to recall the rationales she had lined up and arranged so carefully in her sentences of farewell, I couldn't remember a thing. All I could bring to mind was a woman of middling looks and brains, and what a blessing it was that she was no more than that. What would the circumstances have been like had she been truly pretty or smart or appealing, that woman who had said good-bye to me in a café whose décor consisted of pictures lined up and arranged like careful sentences, with their small, rough seashells, on that evening over which the peace of the country had settled, many years ago?

2

A few days later, though, I found myself frequently coming and going in front of my relative's produce shop. I realized that my mind was dwelling on her, pushed by a strong and compelling desire to know what had happened to her.

It was not just a question of what had happened to her, though, for quite soon I became aware that I did not actually remember much about her. I was startled, for instance, when I realized that I did not recall details, only images drawn in broad and sweeping strokes, portraits wherein I confused her with other women. I had no memory of whether I had actually slept with her or whether circumstances had limited our lovemaking to kissing and some caressing. Sometimes I could see a pair of breasts that I knew belonged to her, but then I would remember that they belonged to someone else. That years had passed did not seem a sufficient excuse for such extreme forgetfulness, especially since she had been the one who had decided to leave, abandoning me in order to settle down among her family and people.

Perhaps, I thought, I have not been in possession of time as I should have been. No doubt she is living in a village somewhere nearby, like most of those who have come here, those who come to wait out the battles going on in the city rather than simply to spend the summer. My pressing curiosity grew in strength; every time I saw her at a distance—and without her seeing me—I summoned disparate fragments of her, collecting them in my memory as I saw what she had become. Her hair had been short then, and darker. Her fingernails had been short as well, and they hadn't been painted. But I could not bring back to mind any memory of a naked body. I didn't understand how this could be, for surely I could not have taken her so lightly as this. No, I couldn't possibly have done that, and so how could my mind play this trick on me? I still had strong and detailed memories of exactly how I had made love to that Italian "artiste," even though I had been dead drunk at the time. I could recall her nakedness perfectly, even to the black beauty mark on her left shoulder. Perhaps I remembered her because she was the only Italian I'd ever laid. Or maybe it was because she'd been my only "artiste."

Of this woman, however, only minor, trivial scenes and images came back to me, and they were no help. I remembered, for instance, her handbag with the clasp that was always broken. I remembered a chipped front tooth in a mouth laughing close to my own. She had gone with me to Samaan's house, conveniently nearby, of that much I was certain; and I had kissed her there, but then what, exactly, had happened afterward? The question kept burning in my mind, confusing and upsetting me. It pressed on me so insistently that I decided I must speak to her. I would go to her, and I would speak.

She did not appear in the least surprised. She greeted me very warmly and by name. Her cheeks took on a pinkish tinge, but she did not act flustered. She said that she was with her husband in his natal village, not far away, where they had gone to flee the strafing along the coast. She always shopped at our village market, she said, because it was larger than the souk in their village and the prices were lower. "Just look at this lovely fruit," she exclaimed, as I helped her carry her bags to the trunk of her car. I stood next to it, uncertain of what to do next. "What a pleasant coincidence," she said, reaching out her hand to shake mine.

On the next occasion she displayed less delight at seeing me. But she acted as though it were perfectly natural for us to come across one another at the spot where we had encountered each other the last time. I helped to carry her sacks of purchases, and when I couldn't find anything to say, I asked her if we could sit together for a little, somewhere, and talk. She made her excuses before I had finished my sentence. She was in a hurry today, she said; maybe next time. "Why not?" she said. "We can find a place to sit, have a coffee, chat." She put out her hand.

That next time—she had not mentioned a particular day—turned out to be the same day of the next week. That made sense. But

I didn't go over to her. I watched her from a distance. My relative helped her load her sacks in the trunk. She paid him and then began to look around, searching for me.

The following week she did not appear. There had been incidents on the road between the two villages, and the route had been closed. The week after that, however, she was there. I did not go near. She did not turn to search for me after paying my relative and setting her bags in the trunk of the car. But then she returned to the shop, to fill new bags, slowly, as if she had forgotten something on her shopping list. I knew that she was prolonging her stay in the shop, thinking that I might show up while she was still there; perhaps I'd been delayed and would even now make an appearance. But I did not go near.

After she had gone, I did not understand why I had not gone near. Why was it that I continued to prefer seeing her like that, from a distance, especially once I knew or at least it appeared to me that she was lingering in the hope that I would appear?

But I was certainly thinking about her. It wasn't that I found anything in particular to dwell on, but I felt her near to me. Just like that, she was there next to me, and that was all. It was a presence that brought neither sadness nor joy; it was simply there. Sometimes it went away, and sometimes it flooded back, settling unstably somewhere in the surrounding air. It no longer bothered me that I couldn't recall the nature of my relationship with her. I wasn't making efforts now to remember her body; I couldn't get any further than a certainty that I had kissed her—a certainty that planted itself within me as soon as my face had come close to hers in the market. This no longer disturbed me, though. That's because what perplexed and bothered me now was the feeling that her cold presence was always nearby, that I was keeping myself from going anywhere near her, and that I preferred to see her at a distance and without her knowledge. Now these were the things that unsettled me.

But then I discovered that I had gotten myself into a much better state, for I no longer had any desire to approach her once again. I was truly much better. After all, what were we going to talk about over our coffee? And where would I have found a spot in which to sit her down and then sit down beside her?

One morning I found myself sitting up in bed at dawn, my eyes wide open and her face there in front of me. Yes, her face was directly in front of mine. I was completely awake, as if I had been up for hours. I felt very confused about what was happening to me. I washed my face and went out, beneath the arbor.

That summer was a hot one, but I kept myself swathed in my cotton coverlet, for in our villages, perched high as they are, the dawn hours are always cold. The fogginess of a summer morning arising in the nearby mountains did not reach far enough to veil the roofs of the villages. My gaze ran among the houses of the hamlet that lay nearby as I tried to guess in which house she might be and how she was sleeping right now, in the peace and lovely freshness of this dawn, lying next to her husband.

3

Now, eyes closed, as I slowly breathe in the fragrance of her neck, I know that everything had to happen as it did. Now I can see that it all had to happen, with the passage of time since she has been here with me, time enough so that my wonder has dwindled, my astonishment that she was there in front of me, my surprise at how quickly it all happened.

It was late one Sunday morning. One of the youths from a neighboring family came by and drank coffee with me. He was distraught; he had to drive down into the city, but he didn't have enough gas in his car. The gasoline supply had been cut off, but he had heard that a station at the edge of the main entrance into our village might be getting a tank delivered just before noon. He asked me if we could go together and wait in the car after parking in front of the station.

As we waited, I caught a glimpse of her passing by, in her car, heading toward the village where she lived. I said to my friend, "Come on, let's go to the next village—there must be gasoline in the gas stations there." But he shrank from the idea. It was impossible, he said. "They might kidnap us. At the very least they'll make fools of us. We are not women! And they will be sure to recognize us."

Suddenly we heard the resounding claps of explosions. We saw smoke rising from bombs falling in the valley nearby. My friend turned the key in the ignition so we could get away, but the car choked before he could get it moving. We got out and dashed over to hide behind the walls of the gas station, knowing how dangerous an explosion the first bit of shrapnel could cause. Then I saw her again, in her car, heading this time in the direction of our village. I ran after her, shouting, and she stopped. I climbed in beside her. As she drove, we could see that bombs were coming down on the road, though they were still a long way in front of us.

We got out of the car and began to climb up into the forested land to the right of the road, to give ourselves the protection of the soaring boulders. Her hand in my grip, I was pulling her because she was very frightened and did not know where I was taking her. She was saying the same words over and over. "But what happened?"

Night fell, and we were still taking the shelter of a high rock. We saw the glowing red missiles colliding in the sky before pouring down onto the two villages and surrounding countryside. Then I found myself holding her tightly, and I became aware that her head was against my chest. I sensed that it was not just fear that held her there.

The roar of the bombs vanished as dawn came. Thinking she was asleep, I made no attempt to disentangle myself so that I could see better. I could feel her regular breathing across my entire body. I wasn't conscious of my own state of mind.

When she stood up straight, stared into the sky, and then looked at me, I figured that she would turn toward the road, where her car waited, and would head home. Instead, she turned around and sat down next to me. I thought about taking her home with me, but I made no move to do so. Then we heard the noise of military vehicles and heavy trucks on the move, a screeching sound, and the firing of bullets. I knew then that we would not be able to break through the barriers that they would have erected along the road. They would not leave us alone to make the crossing now, when everything was tense to the point of hysteria. They would not let us pass, whether in that direction or the opposite. I gazed at her, dizzy and fearful, my eyes unfocused, but an odd sense of well-being taking firm hold within me.

"Come with me," I said to her.

We walked quite a distance before coming to a narrow road that had no outlet. With the din of the violent bombing in my ears, I couldn't concentrate on figuring out where we were. I asked her if she felt hungry, but she didn't answer. She hadn't been talking at all, but she was looking at me all the time. She stared at me constantly. I could tell that she wasn't afraid, even if she stayed so close to me that our bodies touched. It was then that I felt I could shake off my doubts, for clearly she was determined to stay with me. Until that moment I had not dared to ask her if she wanted to go back. And I was no longer afraid of her.

"A car will come by here, it must," I told her. "Come on, let's wait in the shade of the trees." We sat down under the overhanging branches.

"Do you have any more cigarettes?" I asked her. She stretched out her legs and lay her head down on my belly. My chest felt like it would split open as I tried hard not to move. Then I found myself unable to move. I was looking at her face. And then I could not believe what I saw there. I saw my soul before me. . . . She opened her eyes to look at me, and all I saw now was her mouth.

When I kissed her, my body jerked in the empty air. My knees trembled and gave way, and the earth seemed to sink very far beneath me. Her mouth was warm and soft. Liquid. I was pulling her to me so hard that it cut off my breathing and I had to pull back, but I bore down on her mouth once more and obstructed my own breathing all over again.

The smell of her went through my nose and flooded my mouth as if it were hot water. Searing mercury shooting forth, to roll back into a moving, glistening orb that burst out once again so that I had to gather the drops in from wherever they had slid across her body. How easy it all was! That she bent and spiraled and opened to my movements made me feel that for the first time I was leaving behind the weight of my great body. I felt like I had become many men and yet also the shadow of a single man. I was heavy and yet weightless and small as a bird; I was empty and full; I blazed and I bent as if I had no spine, no bones.

It was the first time I penetrated a woman whose body I could not see. Her body, invisible to me, was more a liquid to be swallowed. Her heat within me seemed more powerful, more solid, than any form my eyes could shape. It was like a blindness that released the ultimate reach and power of all my other senses. I saw nothing, no skin, no belly, no thighs.

And so I did not see my desire, either. I did not know what had come upon me. It was as if it all happened in a single instant. In one moment of time—I pulled her to me, I kissed her, came into her, screamed. It was as if what I had done to her, with her, had nothing at all to do with sex, nothing to do with laying women.

When I recall it now, I see other things. Other scenes return to me, the thoughts I had after I stretched out next to her. I studied her face anxiously, for after I came out of her, I knew that I would never come out of her. I was frightened because days and days of screaming and crying and dancing would not contain my joy and my regrets, my assurance of being defeated, my final loss of self. This is a remorse that has no end because such pleasure will not happen again, and because if I want to regain it, I must be with someone else, someone other than myself. And because I will not be able to bear my dependence on what is outside of myself. I will not be able to endure my submission to another body—one that will age, sicken, die, and leave me forever. No one but I may do that. People invented pure love for God because they knew they would never see Him. They did not give Him a body or a death. And God never leaves, for He enters all places that are empty of Him.

I lay full length beside her. Her body had separated from me, returning to its own rhythms that would mesmerize me until, fixed in place, I would corrode and wear away. I was sad—now I know that I was sad—as I stared at the tiny black moles scattered across her flesh, across her face and neck, and noticed short hairs growing between her eyebrows, little black spots on her nose, the edge of her lower lip, a light golden fluff of hair over her upper lip. And a tooth chipped ever so slightly.

Now, now I know the sense of the incredulity I felt then, of the emptiness I felt, of the premonition I had of defeat and ruin.

Seated in the truck that took us away from the little side road, I kept looking at her. At her hands: I examined the thin line of flesh hugging her fingernails. Her fingernails gleamed under a translucent rose-colored polish. I saw the nail of her index finger, beneath it some dirt, which I began to clean with my teeth.

The truck was crowded with folks fleeing from the bombing, among them a woman who would not stop screaming. The other passengers were weeping out of compassion for her, but they were also grumbling that her screaming might guide the bombs toward us. They were saying to her, "Thank your Lord that everyone else is safe."

I heard nothing. But now I remember that the woman was screaming because her nursing son had fallen from her as she was climbing into the truck, which did not wait. She had left him there.

Me, her fingers were in my mouth.

4

We did not stay long in the school building where they had deposited us. I told them that she was my wife, and no one requested her papers. They gave us a mattress, two bedcovers, and a corner of a room that already contained one family—parents, a grandmother, and four children.

We put up a green sheet around our bed. The family did not like us because we wouldn't talk to anyone. We didn't tell our story, and we didn't go along when they went to ask for water and to protest the bad food being handed around to everyone. Also, we managed to get water for ourselves and were able to wash twice; they didn't like that, either.

I would lower the green sheet, put my arms around her, nestle my head into her neck, and breathe deeply.

At night we climbed to the roof of the school building, where many of the school's temporary residents spent the fresh, cool evenings. I wrapped her in the blanket and massaged her feet in my palms until they grew warm. She often got chilled, and her feet always felt clammy, like a couple of fish. It was because she ate so little, I would tell her. But after that I was at a loss, wondering what to talk about. Ideas did not come to me without terrific effort. I would imagine autumn, for instance, and how it would rain heavily then. I could talk about how soft the breeze was; I would point out the stars and recite their names. Then I would go down to the shop they had opened in the administrators' office. I would buy her a box of tea cookies or perhaps a bar of chocolate, which—back on the roof—I pressed her to eat. With a laugh, she would bite into whatever I had brought. Then we would remain there, on the roof, until it had emptied of people, sometimes not until dawn was almost with us. In its emptiness I could kiss her again and again. I could pull her clothes off and sit still, just looking at her. It frightened her. She would glance all round and tug at the edges of the blanket. And I sat still, just looking at her, as if it were the first time. Every time there was something different, new things. She was completely different, but also completely the same as she had been and completely identical to me in my strong desire, every time, to burst into tears. Like an idiot, I said to myself. Here she is, right in front of you, with you. Waiting for you as if you are her lord and master. Whenever you feel desire. And she feels desire, too.

Sometimes I covered her again, draping the blanket over her. Her nakedness was too much for me: the brilliant light of her breasts, the black moon of each nipple—it was more than I could bear. I would wrap the blanket around her and stretch out beside her. I would rub her hair, braid it, undo it, kiss it. That longing would come back to me, a yearning to sob, but it came back slowly, so that I could regain my breath as I stared into the sky. This was stronger than I, too much for me to bear. It was more powerful than all of my capacity and vaster than the area covered by my skin. Lost, I was pulled to her and had no will to resist. I was exhausted, used up, before I could even embrace her—defeated, drained, the palm of my hand drinking in the heat of her bare shoulder, filling me up, drop by drop, from the hollow of my soles . . . I had never been full since the day my mother gave birth to me. I never felt full. Then she would open the blanket and take me to her.

Sometimes she drifted into a light sleep. I would feel at rest, relieved that for now she had forgotten me and would leave me to myself. Inhaling over her mouth, I took in the air that was leaving her, the breaths that had diffused through her body and had purified her blood. For long moments, resting my weight on my arm, I watched the vein in her neck pulse. I envied the blood that ran through her. I did not move, for I wanted her to go on sleeping, so near to me. I wanted her this way, silent and still, and myself alone. I counted her pulse as I saw the vein swell, and carefully I placed my hand there, trying to penetrate through to the hot fluid circling through her, flowing beneath her skin, inside her organs and limbs.

One day she will leave, I would tell myself. Yet I could not imagine her returning to her husband or to her family. I did not envision her becoming weary of me or vexed at me. Simply, I had the certainty of her departure, merely because she was separate from me, apart from me, in another body that she commanded with her own will. Simply, she would stand up and walk in a direction unknown to me. She would command her feet to move, and they would carry her somewhere where I was not, taking one of innumerable possible directions but none of them mine, none of them holding me. She would stand and walk away, and I would stay where I was. And there she might die, away from me, might die just like so very many people who are dying.

There were times when I wanted to scream, "Mama!" as I looked at her sleeping next to me on the roof of the school. Times when I wanted to wake her and dress her in her clothes and ask her, "Where will you go? In what direction will you walk, never to come back?"

I would remind myself that she was a woman, and this always staggered me. It truly amazed me that she had a body that was not my body, a form that did not even look anything like my body. Her body's shape didn't fit mine. I tried to draw patience from time. It will be good enough, I would tell myself, good enough if she stays with me long enough that I learn to bear it. If she stays with me a long time, long enough for time to do its work.

Time cuts like a sword through the things of this world. Passing over, time slices everything in two, and thus time will prove my salvation. Like a powerful and volatile disinfectant, time sterilizes one-half and detaches it from its vital origin. Time will desiccate that half, suck out its mass, render it barren. But it will root itself and live on, while the second half, the remains of it, will rise and scatter with the first puff of wind, to be deposited elsewhere, accumulating in remote places that we do not even know. And so we are freed of those remains. Whatever is given weightlessness, whatever is made sterile, left to scatter and settle where it may—that is what remains, but it lives on only in its sterility. Our bodies remain, in their barrenness, while our thoughts and our powers of memory disperse, fertile, to settle far away. Our bodies, sterilized by time as it passes across them and turns them into identical shapes, will no longer carry anything but a withered, dried-out sex. Thus do objects neutralize and hide their origins. Woman and man become a single form, one body, their organs and limbs fixed into a single sex. A woman grows a light moustache and beard that shadow those of a man. A man develops small and pendulous breasts that mirror a woman's once they have aged and dried out. Even their sex organs come to look like twins in their fragile suspension, their size, and their lightly swelling contours.

Just so are mummies sanitized by the passage of time; the more ancient they are, the purer they are. They preserve themselves in losing their sex, in an aseptic existence without the eggs and the hormones of so long ago. Thus, no parasites can enter them, ever, to infect them. No parasites can enter unless they are hauled from their own time and forced into an age that is not theirs, unless they are disposed of in a different atmosphere.

Time passes across us, my wife and me. And so we will grow to look alike. We will come to have a single body and a single sex, not two. I will bring back her sex, take it upon myself, and bend myself to it. And that will prove my salvation.

But time passes over us, too, like a woman. It slows us down. It fixes us in place, in its place. It sterilizes us before we can even remark the long passage of time. It is a woman who keeps us from the blessing of parasites—and from their mercy.

5

My spells of amnesia have returned, and they visit me often. They return because of their compassion for me. Sometimes when I look at a tree, I can see the sap rising slowly from the moisture-laced ground, rising through the veins in the wood to reach the explosions of green that spread into the leaves. When I look at Sister St. Vincent-de-Paul's belly, I see the whorls of her organ and the rose-colored leafiness of her womb, and I see her tiny eggs, each one forced out to drop like a hazelnut, rolling down a tiny tube and attaching itself beneath a pair of tiny, lush, sprouting plants. When I look at my skin, I see it covered with those microscopic spots of jaundice that the woman deposited on me in the shape of tiny eggs, drawing their nourishment slowly. I see my bones turning white to shine like the bones in museums. Calcium and phosphorus, that's what I see.

My many bouts of forgetting take me into others' realms. I am in the truck as it moves, slithering between fires erupting on both sides, and I start screaming at them to give me back the little one who fell as I climbed up, the little one who stayed behind. I shout at them to stop and retrace their path. I rumple my long hair and declare that time will make no difference to me. What does it mean to say it's impossible to return to a time before he fell away from me? What does it mean that I now exist in a moment long after his fall? I am there, still, and he falls from me; he is still and always on his way to the ground.

Jabir says to me, "Don't let things get any worse for you. Things are good for you right now, they're good for all of us. You have no children who are falling from trucks."

Jabir believes that my condition worsens when I forget. He doesn't realize that forgetting is my chance to get some rest from it all. He doesn't know that my body starts to ache when I let it relax too much. That is because Jabir is not like me. When he comes to Dayr al-Salib, he has already forgotten everything. And when he begins eating and sleeping and the tranquilizers start circling through his blood, he comes back, comes out of his oblivion. Also, he is not like me because even when he has spells of amnesia, he can still remember many things. Sometimes he'll tell me things like that, laughing at himself. He gets a little embarrassed about what he has put his family through.

After that dream, he told me (and he was always postponing telling me what the dream actually was), he started losing sleep and finding that he could not eat. He went on for days without food or sleep, without going to work. He stayed absolutely silent and hated having any sort of noise or commotion around him. He didn't know what time of day or night it was and would not let his wife or children speak to him.

"And then," he told me, "one day, when I was standing on the balcony, I leaned out and began to stare at the apartments nearby. All those people, I asked myself—what are all they doing? The question kept pressing on me. What are they doing? They're all in tiny, cramped apartments, just like me. They've left their houses and have moved into these apartments that were furnished in the first place to receive tourists, businessmen, pimps, and prostitutes, either Lebanese girls or ones from abroad. Look now at how ugly these apartments are. Look—laundry hanging off balconies, all these kids, cooking odors, cockroaches, and rats. They eat and sleep and piss. But what are they all doing? Then I shouted from the edge of the balcony: 'What are you all doing? I want to know, tell me right now. What are you doing, when evil is surging through the streets and alleys as if it's a tremendous flow of lava pouring from a live volcano? Tomorrow you will be annihilated, and no one will be spared. I am the Messiah! The Mahdi!* I will let nothing remain, nor will I appear. In a flood of fire and sulfur will I obliterate you.' I started screaming, 'God is the greatest. *Allahu akbar.* God is the greatest. I will establish justice. *Allahu akbar!*'

"Hands, many of them, arms, came round my body. They pulled me inside. My wife started to cry, and Abu Isam slapped me until I calmed down. He said to my children, 'Don't let it scare you. It's just a seizure and it will pass. His nerves are gone.'

"A few days later the doctor told them that medicine would not do any good. 'You must take him to the eastern sector of the city, take him over to the Christians, to Dayr al-Salib. Here it's impossible; there's nothing we can do. I'll request an ambulance for you from the Red Cross when you've made up your minds.'

"Even now," said Jabir, "I can't stop the shivering in my body when I remember the dream I did not have the strength to tell. I burst

---

*In the Muslim Shi'i tradition, "the Mahdi" refers to the occulted imam, who is expected to return to lead the Shi'i community. [Trans.]

out sobbing every time it comes back to me, even if just a single image from it goes through my head."

One day Jabir did tell me his dream. "I was gathering wheat in the common land in my village when suddenly night fell, a very dark night. I realized that I was alone, on a hill, far above the plain. The sky split to reveal a strong light, and I saw Our Lady Maryam within it, gliding downward toward me. I went down on my knees; I was very afraid, and I asked forgiveness. But she called me by name and put out her hand to me. I reached my hand out, and when the tips of my fingers touched the tips of hers, the mound on which I knelt was all that remained of the world. And beneath me there was only an enormous chasm, only emptiness. From that terrible emptiness there rose music, beautiful and strong, getting grander and fiercer as I listened.

"I woke up and found I was covered in my own piss. The flesh on my chest and shoulders was trembling, from fright, joy. . ."

Jabir looked at me then. "How would you interpret this dream?" he asked me. "No one's been able to get it out of my mind, and they haven't been able to budge my deep faith that I can do something to end this war. I'm not saying that I'll redeem the whole world, just that I'll end the war. I don't dare to say this to anyone but you because you are my friend."

"Right, the Virgin Mary, Jabir," I said to him. "I have my own story with her, and I'll tell you that story some other time. What I think is that you had your dream after you'd been cursing the Messiah and his mother plenty, and you got scared. You were afraid, and you saw evil, devils playing in the street under the balcony of your home."

"But I did not curse the Messiah," protested Jabir. "That's Issa you're talking about, man, how could I do that when Our Lady Maryam is his mother?* It wouldn't happen!"

"Never mind, Jabir," I said. "Never mind. You must eat well and sleep soundly if you want to return to your family."

After Jabir told me his dream, he began giving me furtive glances. And if we were in the garden at the same time, he rarely came over to me. In fact, he didn't approach me at all unless he was with nurses. If

*Issa is the Arabic version of Jesus, whom Muslims revere as a prophet. [Trans.]

they had assigned him a chore and he refused to do it, they would complain about him in my hearing and then go off, leaving him to stay a little with me.

Jabir unnerves me with his weakness, his hapless manner, his mental lapses, and the way he refuses to eat in the canteen when I'm there. When he acts like that, I hate him. I really detested him when I realized that he wanted me to love him, to believe him and to talk to him, and to let him pal around with me. I knew then that he was lying, that he lies a lot. That dream of his is made up, I realized, the whole thing is a web of lies.

Jabir is lying when he says that I am the only one he can tell, for this dream of his has a particular task to perform, and its meaning is as clear as the day. Jabir tells it to everyone in order to protect himself because he is constantly aware that he is in the eastern sector, and he knows exactly why they mock him in the bath. Jabir lies and invents because he is weak and wants to protect himself. He reminds me of Samaan.

Samaan. I cried when I said good-bye to him at the airport. He had decided to go to Germany, where his cousin is. He said to me, "I'm not capable of being a killer. I tried, and I couldn't do it. I peed in my clothes, and my clumsiness almost killed me. I'll finish my studies in Germany. I'm not a fighter. Write to me, don't forget me." Samaan, at whose house I used to sleep more often than I did at my own: Samaan said all of that to me.

Samaan. I cried again when I met him at the airport two years later; I wept at the sight of his unfocused eyes and his sickly pallor. For a few, sleepless days he refused to say anything, but then he told me that an international espionage and crime outfit was after him. After a few more days he told me why. It was because he had taken on important responsibilities in the sect he had embraced in Germany. It was a universal religion, and he held the rank of minister. More days, and he let on that it was the German woman with whom he had fallen in love and had married who had denounced him to the dangerous organization because he was tracking her to get her back. Then he insisted that the money he had spent on her was the cause of his mother's death, rather than the cancer, because he had ignored her pleas for money to get medical treatment, spending it all instead on the German woman whom he'd loved and married. Her father owned a great factory, and she was rich and spoiled. Finally he told me that he would have killed her if she hadn't exposed him to the organization first.

"Never mind," I comforted Samaan. "There are plenty of weapons here. We'll just go back to Germany and kill her. And the crime people won't know what we are up to because we'll disguise ourselves and forge passports. It's possible, even easy, to do that. It doesn't even cost very much."

After Samaan had started eating and sleeping, I took him to his mother's grave. I wouldn't leave him by himself for a minute. After he met Mona and began smiling again, I was reassured to see that his eyes no longer looked dull and unfocused. I could tell that he was sleeping like a child, and my mind was finally at rest about him.

But Samaan went on needing me. He demanded his friends' presence, all of us, constantly. He was always sliding into minor nervous breakdowns and then popping tranquilizers. We believed he would commit suicide and lived in fear of that possibility. The specter of it was a personal threat to each of us, but especially so to me. I couldn't imagine what my mental condition would be like if Samaan were to kill himself.

Things went on like this. I made allowances for whatever he did and gave him free rein. Samaan was my spoiled child. My sole condition was that he must go on breathing. And sleeping.

And then one day my eyes suddenly opened to the fact that Samaan had married Mona. And had a daughter. And owned a home. He had not missed a day of work. He had very good relations with everyone around him, for everyone was kind to Samaan. But Samaan always wanted more, and he romped like a pleased puppy in our love and care. On that same day I also awoke to the fact that I had not gotten married; that I did not have a home, even a rented one; that I had no permanent job, and everyone considered me an annoyance—backward, insolent, violent, clumsy, and completely untalented. And they found me unpleasantly strong, brutal, and aggressive. Repellent. Uncontained. Always too much. I became conscious that I was alone and that the image they had sketched of me was true. I knew then that

I hated them all. I had no woman and no place of my own, and my heart hung in the empty box of my chest by a mere cotton thread. So I took on the image they had decreed. I imposed myself, the annoyance that was me.

I was the strongest of all of them, and the most belligerent, whether aggression was called for or not. No one saw that I stood like a crumbling spear, like a thorn dried out from the inside, that I was alone—contrary, insolent, stubborn, hateful. No one saw me. I held myself there, erect. They started to meet without me. They intrigued around me, mocked my life, forgave their own betrayals with compassion and indulgent understanding, but I remembered every one resentfully. I was unbending. They began cooperating, exchanging all kinds of services. They spent evenings together and did everything collectively, on the sly. I stayed on my feet, though, obstinate as a mule in my stance, while they continued on, escorted by their plaints and grievances about the bad times. They regarded their own weaknesses and Samaan's limitations benevolently. They told lie after lie. I stayed firm, and their behavior made me feel stronger. They just went on and on, lying and deceiving themselves, while I stood tall, like a crumbling spear in a strong wind.

Samaan loathed me and began to avoid me. At night I would say to him, "Samaan, how can you forget me and ignore me and let yourself be drawn into their stupid little treacheries, all of these lies that you toss back and forth? We weren't like this before the wars. Samaan!"

Take care, Jabir. All of you—watch that you do not come to like me, to stick with me, to inhale the same air. Watch yourselves because I'll come back to you repulsive, harmful, wicked, and totally without sympathy. Guard against approaching me and loving me, for I see the sap rising slowly from the soil that sends moisture into the capillaries inside the green wood, rising to the pale green eruptions in the leaves. Sometimes that is what I see.

6

I was the dung beetle of the desert, the drinker of dust. I was all of that for her.

Endless distances, one horizon extending into the next, and a crimson surface of fire, never still; an immense sun, low in the sky; broiling air, sucked in and expelled in a single movement, sparked by the touch of the fire as it envelops and entangles and unites. Sand that pops, explodes, and shatters into smaller grains.

Knowing it is the will of the Lord, the dung beetle of the desert awaits the hours of the Lord. Barely before dawn, the grayish twilight will pass, and the fog will fall, thickening and sinking onto the sand.

The dung beetle of the desert expands inside of his own body. He swells without unrolling his limbs, and without puffing up with the moisture, for he must preserve his own internal heat at a temperature as deeply contrasting as possible with the coldness of the hour. He draws himself into a tiny bundle, his legs bunching in the sand, settles himself in his little body, and leans on it, tucking his head underneath so that he is as vertical as can be to the ground. He seals all of his orifices, and all along his body the fog moves, depositing its dew to form tiny beads of moisture that gather into droplets. They slip down his skin, underneath to his mouth, and he drinks.

But I did not understand the wisdom of the Lord. What wisdom was it that He gave to the desert its own dung beetle? Why? If it is a desert, a place of thirst and silence, a visible and cautionary reminder of death and stillness, why did He offer it His dung beetle? Why did He condemn His dung beetle to a life of viciousness, torment, and permanent discomfort? Was it so that the beetle would know thirst every hour of the day and would work to conceal itself from the very place in and for which it was created, a place hardly meant for the living? Of its own location the dung beetle of the desert knows only the meaning of flight from it and the moments of fog that pass swiftly along the ground so that it may drink. It sees the desert as an imaginary and fleeting imprint of reality, an image it smuggles into its own existence . . . escaping into its own night when the desert is once again desert—when the desert's daytime emerges and the beetle can find nowhere to live. It knows only the facets of the desert that are forbidden to it, knows through half-caught apprehensions, intuition, fear. It knows instinctually those things about the desert that will kill it. Were it not for the dung beetle's fear and its flight into the deceptive, artificial night that it knows to create, it would believe that the desert is that immense wellspring that floods downward from the sky to cover its existence in coolness and tranquility.

Why is the dung beetle of the desert not in the woods instead? Why is it not grazing happily with its brothers, the forest dung beetles, who know the forest intimately, for they can spend all day and night exploring? Their day is the forest's day, their night is its night. Whenever the fancy takes them, they can drink from the running spring or from the rain that they can rely on in season and at other times, too, or from the dew that spreads across the soft and pliant greenery. Why are the desert dung beetles not among the creatures that spend their existence singing and chirping, instead of sinking their heads into the ground to drink the sweat of their own bodies or the fog of a capriciously merciful sky before scurrying toward a willed oblivion to hide even from nature, their mother?

But the wisdom of the Lord shows no love for the dung beetle of the desert, except insofar as it serves as an exemplary warning of the Lord's fearsome command to whosoever will heed the lesson, an example of His inimitable power to produce life in all its variety of type and environment, and even in the teeth of death. It is like unto Divine wisdom's affection for those peoples who—in their ability to survive—create forage for the hungry imagination of the peoples of the forests and farmlands, a fertilizer to nourish the blessed survival instinct, and a lesson for their dull, slothful, vainglorious minds. Observe the desert dung beetle; take heed of the peoples who make civil wars. Watch as the prophet Ayyub takes the sated worm that has fallen from his wound. Ayyub—Job—patiently replaces the worm inside once again.

But I did not say to her: observe me. The air I breathed was burnt to ash, the ground around me was shorn, and I possessed nothing: I had no one for myself. Yet, secretly, my head tucked beneath, my bulk unfolding to its furthest extent, with my sparse memory and my impoverished imagination I was adjusting my orifices precisely to my solitude and estrangement, that for her I might hunt down the fog, erecting traps to catch it so it would remain suspended, so it would hang upon me, and then it would slip over me so that she might drink.

Saddened, I sit motionless, pondering how to catch and hold air that is fierce, that burns and poisons, is vacuous and deceptive; how to suck from it a moisture that collects on my skin, beading there so that she will find my skin glowing and fresh, tender, supple, and she will accept it gladly.

How can I amuse and divert her, make her forget, let the time pass, so that she will stay on? How, when I know that no one loves me for very long? Not a single person has loved me for any length of time, long enough that my lust, so like a leech, drinks until it is ready to drop off on its own, sated. Me and the others—we never get it wrong. With the intuition of hunted animals, we know the pit lies before us, signifying our death. No one has loved me long enough for me to turn back from the distance I have put between us, to search for the lover who has remained at the verge of the path, with oozing wounds, still, like the Good Samaritan, still there and loving me.

I know that she loves me.

I know how she closes her eyes when I come so near she can smell me; like a blind but rambunctious puppy, she'll sniff me and breathe in my scent. I know how she'll open her mouth for me, her arms, her thighs; she absents herself, inert, so that it is my presence that commands our desire. I know how she'll moisten me, how she'll freshen me with her saliva and launch her breath over me until I am an interval of coolness in the heat. How she kisses my hands and leans her face against my open palm before she sleeps—I know all of that. And then she will sleep.

She loves me, I know that.

Whenever I begin to eat, she stops and watches me. She smiles and gazes as if she herself is guiding the bite on its route from my mouth and throat until it has turned into nourishment circulating through my blood and organs. She stops eating and watches, as if I'm growing larger before her eyes and at that very moment taking on the energy and strength of the man who I am. When she finds that I am getting confused and embarrassed, she averts her gaze. She eats with me until I am finished. She carries the food away and comes back to me to wash my fingers in the saliva of her mouth. She opens my shirt, puts her face to my chest and tells me to breathe slowly, to try to fall asleep, so that she can harmonize the rhythm of her breathing to the movement of my chest.

She is opening my crossed arms to put her lips at the inner crease of my elbow where the skin is tender and the veins protrude, warm. She presses on my arm to better see the veins and then returns with her lips to the crease in the fold and stays there, buried in the skin that offers a child's likeness. Perhaps that is the part of me that will not age and sag, perhaps it will stay as it is now, even years after she has left me and I have become an old man.

After she came home with me to the village and settled in with us, it did not fluster her, when the water was cut off, to walk slowly over to the little basin in full view of Asmaa. Kneeling to help me wash my feet as she fixed me with her eyes, she would raise my hands from the water as if in a pose of entreaty. Asmaa, uncomfortable, would leave the room. But she would simply soap her hands well and begin to rub them over my feet. "Don't be embarrassed," she'd say. "I love your feet as I love your hands and your heart. Tomorrow, if you like, you can wash my feet . . . or you can wash all of me."

I see her pouring clean water over my feet. She lifts them into the towel in her lap. She dries them slowly, carefully, as if she knows there's an ache inside them. She smiles again. "Stretch them out, don't be shy. You are my master, and also my servant; my disciple and my messenger and my prophet. Do as Jesus did. Extend them and don't be self-conscious. I love your feet as much as I love your heart." She rubs them, telling me that if your feet are relaxed and rested, then your whole body is at rest—and your soul, too, because your feet are at the very end of you. They are where all the threads of you are knotted together. She smooths the flowing hair, kisses my feet at the soft, naked space above the toes, and walks away, hoisting the basin to the sink.

Asmaa always told people that *she* was an old friend who had come for a long visit. She had gotten caught in our area by the troubles, but presently she would return home. Then Asmaa changed her story, explaining that she was actually from our area originally and was a Christian, like us, but all her folks had died, and so now she would live with us. Later, Asmaa began saying that she was my fiancée, that her folks had gone to live far away from their homeland, and that we would get married when her family came back from Australia to bless the marriage. Asmaa knew nothing about her; at least, Asmaa did not know that she already had a husband. But the family and the neighbors, hearing her explanations, went off satisfied to their own cares and occupations or to other amusements.

Asmaa was perfectly willing to avoid showering her with questions, for she realized that we loved each other and knew that this woman was mine—she was my woman, whether or not she was a wife. Though Asmaa hid it from me—and from her—she was profoundly uneasy about the arrangement and afraid for me. Still, after a while she did come to feel affection for my woman, perhaps because she loved me. Or maybe it stemmed from the love that my unmarried sister had never herself known and about which she had so often heard news and tales, and for such a very long time.

7

I know that she loves me, but nothing is enough to satisfy me. Nothing suffices for me. Nothing is enough to fill me with certainty.

The more she loved me, the vaster she seemed to be and the farther beyond my embrace I felt she was. As she encompassed more, so I shrank. I became smaller and weaker, so diminished that I felt helpless. I became confused about everything, and sometimes I wasn't able even to sleep with her. I asked myself how this could possibly happen. How can she possibly love me in any moment but this very one? How can I make sure that the desire she feels is something more than a restless discontent, caprice, a question of mood, since it has not been put to a test?

The more I saw her loving me, the weaker I became and the more muddled and inept I was about everything in my life. A strong desire grew in me to put her to the test. . . .

I'll leave her alone in the house while I go out, I decided. I'll leave, but I'll return almost at once, surreptitiously, to see what she might be doing in my absence, how she reins in her restlessness, how she handles her loneliness when I am not there. She is not aware of it, but I can see her sitting with Asmaa on the stone bench outside the house, under the arbor, the two of them moving solidly into middle age; she even has Asmaa's spinsterlike aspect, sitting in the state of virginity that has hardened around my sister. She helps Asmaa open the ripe apricots and spread them out on the pallets and trays that they will place around the edges of the terrace, under the eye of the sun, which is beginning to cool down and drop heavily in a faltering September. The pair of them move slowly, their minds wandering, little smiles on their faces. I am squatting in the tiny vegetable garden behind the pots of dahlias, and in the gloom I watch her closely as she cleans her fingernails—now once again as short as they used to be—of the stickiness from the apricots. With her forearm she shoves her light locks of hair back from her brow. I notice once again that she is not pretty. And that she is remote; she's from elsewhere. She is different, other; she is not someone connected to me. I remember that occasionally I have to explain some of our words whose meanings in our dialect she does not understand.

She doesn't glance at her watch or turn her eyes to the front door. She interlaces her hands in her lap and in the faint light of the terrace watches the movement of little night creatures: the flight of the tiny butterflies and the evening insects that make the drizzles of light flicker and move. She remains there alone after Asmaa has gotten up and gone inside and the smells of dinner have begun to seep through the windows. Seeing her alone and far away, I ask myself what this woman wants—this woman who shows no appearance of waiting for me. She seems to be enjoying something, but what is it? And what is she thinking about? Who is she thinking about? How can you know what circles through a woman's head, as like as it is to the crop of a bird, tossing moods and oscillating images? How do you know what goes through her head when she is alone, and where can you find the certainty of it?

I stay in my hiding place until I feel bored, irritated, tired. I decide to go out and stay out the entire night so I can see how it will affect her. I walk through the thicket near the house and begin to search for a pal with whom I can spend the time—a man who just by his presence will inadvertently strengthen my resolve, who will stand by me and take my part against her, who will talk to me so I can forget and see her as nothing but a minor part of life, just one among many things, just a woman whose possession they envy. A man to talk with me and return her image to its place among all the images of the many women that our evening conversations touch upon when we get bored of politics and news of the power cuts. When there come to us thoughts of fruit and we sense the dryness of our mouths. A man who will relieve me without talking about her, will soothe me by talking about other women. All at once I'll remember that they all look alike. Then I can tell myself that I'll go back to her now just as he will return to his wife.

They never mention her to me; if they do, I shut those doors quickly, and they understand. But at the end of the night I'm gripped by a vague sympathy for her. On my way home I start a silent conversation with her, threatening to punish her if I find her asleep rather than awaiting my return . . I see the light of the candle seeping from under the door to the room. Going in, I see her sitting in bed, lifting her head to meet my gaze as I enter.

I stand still, looking at her. I have the impression that, seeing me, she is shaking off a light sadness. I ask her why she hasn't gone to sleep, but she doesn't answer. She is sitting on the edge of the bed, near me. I step over to the window, undo the buttons on my shirt, and stare into the blue depths of the night. I resolve not to sleep with her. Not tonight, and not for many nights to come. I think about the narrow mattress outside, on the terrace, as I inhale the scent of her shadow trembling on the wall before me. But when I hear the sigh of her bare feet on the floor, padding over to where I stand, my knees go limp and I fold. She lifts the back of my shirt and swathes my naked skin in her arms as if they are a belt of rough skin. Her hot mouth moves up my back to my neck. She presses her body against me, and I can see her. I see her flesh falling back now as if she is lying flat on her back, her breasts flattening outward, her belly stretching, slightly hollowed, the paired mounds of her small pelvis rising slightly. I see her body's curves against me, intertwined in me, hot.

Panting, I take her, standing. It is not an unquenchable ardor, not overwhelming desire or lovesick passion. For I am blind. I see only blackness, thick and impenetrable. She rises up from within me like my soul, like my final breath of life. And my laugh is like the laugh of the possessed when I stare into the mirror and do not see her.

I know this as I stare at her face afterward. Her eyes are closed, but they are looking at me. She holds me tightly, holds me against her; she does not want me to come out of her. But where is she?

Where shall I place her, this woman who does not resemble me and yet who is to such a great extent my self? I don't see women. When I notice a woman on the street, it is a woman who is nothing like her but rather has more in common with men. I realize, when I think about it, that I see only women who are unlike her and who resemble men. It is as if the sex she bears is against me, and I despise it. I want it to stop with her, to be hers alone. Or perhaps it makes me miserable to realize that she is so very unlike me. I want her to come to me so that I can bear her and so that she will understand how jagged and quick to break apart I am, here in my heavy body, whose size and weight and sluggishness command me.

I began to appreciate whatever seemed to verge on my reluctant virility and looked likely to appease me for it. With envy I heard of animals and plants that self-reproduce, having both male and female organs: a sex liberated from pain. In whatever pleased or attracted me I looked hard to find unremitting partiality toward the confines of equivocation, ambiguity, and doubt.

Perhaps this is why I always loved the sight of the froth over her upper lip, which had regained its blackish tinge, and the eyebrow hairs that had grown out so that they intertwined lightly over her nose; she did not pluck them out. And her fingernails, clipped down to the flesh, without polish, and the veins of her hands blue and swelling.

This is why, I knew, I can listen so intently to Umm Kulthum, why her songs enchant me so.* She is not a feminine singer, not at all. Her face lacks the prettiness appropriate to a woman's face, and her lungs are extraordinarily large. Her breasts are massive, true; but her neck is thick as it encases her enormous throat. She draws me, too, be-

*Umm Kulthum (1908–75) of Egypt remains one of the Arab world's most celebrated and beloved singers. [Trans.]

cause her voice encompasses more than one sex, soaring high as the dome of the womb and falling as low as the well of the testicles. Her voice is saltiness and sweetness—an asexual voice, but a bisexual one, too. The lyrics to her songs are in a masculine voice, but one that encompasses the feminine. She is even called *"The* Lady." That's all, just *al-sitt,* "The Lady," as if to confirm all that is uncertain, equivocal, undecided; as if to decide once and for all, both to escape and to contain any remaining confusion. She shows no hesitations about furtive conversations, lyrical flirtations . . . she tells of nights of passion and communion, of goblets of wine passed round, of the mouth of the beloved. Women hear her as a man, and men hear her as a woman. Her voice offers the anger of a woman and the resignation of a man. Her voice is the exchange of lovers.

The tempo of Umm Kulthum's voice hovers between the femininity of a waning aristocracy and the masculinity of an emerging liberation, between the elderly and the adolescent. The physiology of her voice is a careful carding and blending of hormonal balance, yet also a parting, between the public street and the closed wooden balconies of the harem shaded by jasmine, between the sunshine of crowded thoroughfares and the tremor of fresh, hot vapors in the Turkish baths, between sparks flying off red-hot metal and cool milk curdling slowly in warm air. It's the voice simultaneously of a woman and a man. Don't they say something about her being a lesbian?

I know that my woman loves me, but nothing is enough for me, nothing fills me with certainty. How can you know what goes around in the head of a woman when you know that her mind jumps and skips like a grasshopper?

8

Tell me, nurse, what is the sickness from which we suffer? What has made us ill?

The nurse took the lame woman by the hand, helped her gently to sit down, and pushed the kerchief that had slipped down over her eyes back over her hair. He arranged the blanket neatly over her knees and placed her hands on top. It was time for a visit.

They are coming to see this sweet-natured woman for the last time because she is dying, I told myself. I can tell them easily, with one glance—those whom death will reach soon—even though they do not give visible signs or clear signals. My heart merely goes straight to them; my eyes engage them and hold them fast; and I feel a pressing desire to be near them, to examine their features, and to say a word of farewell.

They brought her bananas. They chose bananas because bananas are soft and pasty, easy to peel, and there is no need for sharp knives. Because these people don't think that invalids have anything to do with real life, because they believe that we exist in its shadows, in its unreality, on its remote and barren margins. From us they expect no desire for life, and they even are ready to see an aversion to living on, a withdrawal from life and continual attempts to leave it, whether de-liberately or inadvertently. They believe that life offers us no pleasure because, after all, we must not know it in its reality and its fullness, and because the pallid blood that runs through our veins cannot be ade-quate to sustain life. Our bodies, they believe, are not sufficient—not sufficiently alive—to keep us apace with the caravan of life. Life, they believe, goes on in another place, somewhere other than the body, whereas we, they think, exist in that obscure and ephemeral realm that divides life from death. Somehow, our bodies hang on to life by a barely visible thread that will undoubtedly snap even if there is no ap-parent reason. Or perhaps they think we have an unarguable death wish. We will slip toward death naturally or inadvertently. But this is *their* desire, theirs, for they see us as unworthy of life, undeserving of its charms and even of its harms. They see our vegetative life as not even on a par with that of animals or plants whose existence unfolds according to a predestined plan. Animals and plants do not try to ex-ceed what is expected of them, nor are they anything like people. Yet we do remind these people awfully of themselves. Our bodies are like theirs; like them we walk and talk, and in our pasts we were just like them, before we arrived at our present state, broken, ill, far removed from life and its brilliant essence. Perhaps it is this resemblance that depletes us; perhaps it is because of this that we send fear into their hidden depths, sprinkling water over the seeds of their desire to slip away, to let go, to remain unaware, and to sleep away the days.

They make up their minds to put us at a distance, to put us by ourselves. Then they isolate us in places surrounded by walls and thickets and trees. Maybe that is the reason why, when they speak to us, they raise their voices so much: then they can reach us in the remote locations where they have put us. They talk about us in our presence even if we are fully conscious; they assume we are deaf and unaware in spite of our presence and reality. They say the same phrases again and again, and they are always asking themselves out loud whether we recognize them. After all, they would prefer that we not remember them so that they need not remember us once they have returned home. And we will help them with this. We do help them with it.

Gently they feed her bananas and talk about her when she is right there in front of them. Then, turning to her, they raise their voices to ask easy questions that they repeat without waiting for answers. She has stopped answering, anyway, absorbed in chewing and swallowing, turning away from them. She turns her face away from them.

A mentally ill woman, they think, is sicker than a man who is mentally ill. She is submerged more deeply in her illness, that is, and is more remote, though not necessarily any weaker. She is more likely to do something shameful or scandalous, if she has been put in charge of her own body, for she has no sense of modesty. To her the parts of her body are all alike; she does not control any of them as she ought. It's as if a woman who is mentally ill loses control twice: once because of her instinctual drives and again because she has lost what she was taught to control through carefully contained behavior.

Gently they feed her bananas and clean even the places that she has not soiled. They are apprehensive of her, uneasy about everything. They don't stay long because they assume that she doesn't have any sense of time. The interval between their visits grows longer, and when she dies, they will not be there. They will request the hospital administration to transport her with the aid of a Red Cross van, whereupon they will meet her at an intersection to be determined, one that is not very far from the spot where they will bury her. They won't grieve much because it is her second death. Those who come to pay condolences will tell them she is now at rest. She has died the death of her Lord, a natural death, and the war did not darken her life.

All this I see. I don't know if I am any less sick than she is. I don't know whether those who move about me can also see what I see. Or whether they are sicker than I or less so. I don't know how to classify them, how to assign them to categories, but I can tell the distance between me and those who come to visit us, between invalids and physicians. But between me and those who are outside the walls that lie behind the woods of Dayr al-Salib I cannot measure the distance.

When I encountered Jabir in the meetings the new doctor held, I could not remember how long it had been since I had seen him.

This new doctor must have been living abroad, I told myself, somewhere in America or Europe. And one day he was struck by a kind of zeal. The voice of his nation's conscience pierced him, or the voice of humanity, just as a speeding car is thrown off balance by a blowout in one tire. I do not want money or glory either, he would have told himself. My country needs me because that is where misery abides—true misery and madness. He confronted his foreign wife with making an immediate and irrevocable decision: stay here or return there with me. On a specific and very dark night he packed his suitcases and came to us. He came to us here in Dayr al-Salib, one eye shut by his swelling compassion and the other one blazing with the ardor of his accomplishment, the patient and careful work he would perform to cure us of our diseases of the soul and of society.

Society . . . society . . . Jabir and I burst into laughter in the sessions of the new doctor whenever we heard the word *society*. Every time this happened, the doctor waited for us to recover from our bout of howls and giggles before asking us what it was that roused such a quantity of laughter when we heard the word *society*—whereupon Jabir and I would dissolve into our laughing fit once again. This time our laughing spell would last longer and feel deeper, richer, and more amusing, and it would go on until we were worn out completely and the doctor was in despair. By then the others would have joined in, too. Or they would have gotten bored enough to get up and go off, each to his own pursuits, and it would be awkward to round us all up and start over.

Finally the new doctor had the idea of dispensing with *society*. He began to replace it with *people* and *peers* and *the world outside*. But the session's members—as Jabir and I labeled them—sometimes found the expression advantageous, thinking it would make a good impression on the doctor, and things would get out of hand again. One time the doctor asked us what we would like to substitute for *society*. Jabir responded, "Why substitute anything? We really like it—it makes us happy." When the doctor insisted, we told him that if he wished, he could use *nation* or *nationals* or *populace*. Then we all agreed to find a neutral and formal term like those that doctors use, and we began to say "the people out there."

But the real truth of the matter is that we no longer said anything because we—Jabir and I—really did not participate in those sessions. Jabir, okay, now and then, but I got exasperated after a time, tired of listening to the others' chatter, the questions and the responses, the tiny and depressing dramas. I began to ask myself whether this man was enjoying himself at their expense. Why didn't he leave them alone? What was he trying to get them to understand? He appeared to me sadistic as well as ungrounded; he seemed to come from another world, a different and unreal one. He was glib; he didn't know anything about us. He was intractable, too, and harsh, even perverse, and he harbored something corrupt, stealthy; his scorn for us was not hidden at all, nor was it even tempered by the seasonal mercy that the nurses at least showed toward us. Sometimes he was harder and more wounding than the fighters outside the walls that enclosed the grounds. I do know that I have a tendency to exaggerate sometimes.

I see him open his notebook, holding his tamped-out pipe between thin, pale fingers. He smiles to communicate serene interior nobility; his eyes are keen, and they pierce you. He speaks slowly, making his voice sound meaningful and full of intent. His voice is low, patient, replete with understanding. He begins writing down his observations. He writes in a foreign script.

Once he asked me why I wouldn't speak up. I didn't answer. He tried again. "What's your opinion of what your friend had to say?"

"He isn't my friend," I said. "And I don't have an opinion."

"What would you like to talk about?" he asked. I was silent. He repeated his question, and I cursed at him. "Either leave me alone or go to h——!"

He stared at me with that smile still on his face.

"I don't want to come to these meetings of yours," I said.

"Indeed you will attend my meetings," he responded. I got up, picked up my chair, and swung it at him. He returned the blow skillfully and lightly, rotating my arm into a painful position. I knew then that I hated him to the core and would kill him if I could. I began to dream stray bullets for him, at least when I didn't forget his existence completely.

It must have been after this encounter that I no longer saw Jabir much at all. Perhaps my announced hatred for the new doctor induced Jabir to avoid me. I've forgotten. Perhaps he was with his family for a long spell at that point. I don't remember. But, sitting in my room, I would remember now and then that I wasn't seeing Jabir around, that I hadn't seen him for a long time.

After a while I found myself in those sessions again. I was more worn down by this time and less able to summon my loathing for the new doctor. He started to accept my ongoing silence, my lack of response to him. Once he said to me, "Be aggressive when you feel the urge to be so. It's all right, don't be afraid—I won't get angry at you."

"Don't talk to me like that," I said. "I'm not a child. You'd be better off realizing that I do not like to talk or to sit with others. With *society*."

He didn't respond. But he continued to call me to the sessions, though during them he ignored me. I ignored him, too.

Once he seated me at a table by myself. He gave me some paper and pens and told me to write or draw. "Doodle as you like—whatever comes to you. I'll leave you on your own for now."

Oh Lord. This was all I was lacking.

This is all that was lacking for the Lord's flock, unloved as it is by Him: to write and to draw. This is all we were lacking: little houses roofed in tiles, green and well-shaped trees, and a white dove bearing an olive branch, fluttering gracefully below the sun's orange disc with its carefully straight rays. Exhibitions of our drawings—ours, the raving, the disabled, and the children.

In the midst of their war those blessed folk produce for us a peace that suits us. They concoct a little girl named Rémi.* Her name echoes the name of the suffering orphaned boy in Hector Malot's novel *Without Family*,† known all over the world. Rémi, without family, deprived of a homeland, never knowing peace. Rémi wears a thin, tattered, and innocently pure white dress. Around her the children gather, and at their heart she turns, an airborne being without wings. She is a woebegone orphaned angel, her gestures choreographed by a clever director, son of a people distinguished by a sharp intelligence, celebrated for that extraordinary acumen that God so rarely grants to creatures of this region . . . or even to those of other regions. Around her the children gather—the innocent ones, victims of war, of strife—and form a circle as she moves quietly among them, treating them as softly as if she is a seasoned artist in her fifties. A unique and extraordinary people, this; and its children are victims. *They corrupt the very seed in the earth.* We ruin the seed that lies in the memory of the species, of the fruit, before it even buds; we corrupt it before it can realize its intention to bud. Always we are the pioneers. Of a new awakening, of a renaissance so notable that with it we can end the century: there will follow us other countries, other regions, other cities, here, there, and far away, over there. What we craft today will be reproduced to an astonishing degree, on screens and in books, on maps and in cassettes. Wait a little, and you will see how peoples and secure borders stabilized in arrogance will explode, how we will insert a new alphabet into a new era. A different era, a glorious one. Peoples and nations and cities whose names have not yet been heard will appear. You shall see.

"Sit by yourself—you were a hostage, and they tortured you. Take your time. Be witness to the violence." This is what the doctor says to me. You, whose body erupts in violence, whose head flares

*"Rémi" refers to a young Lebanese singer who was known for the song "Give Us Peace," about the innocence of children martyred by war. [Trans.]

†Hector Malot (1830–1907) was a popular and prolific French fiction writer whose works tended to the melodramatic; his famous *Sans famille* (1878) was aimed at youth and has since reappeared and been translated. [Trans.]

with the memory of killing and the desire to kill again and again, with no limit, no end. Draw, write. Doodle.

Draw a white dove from whose wings fall beads of red. Or a green branch. We will bathe you and comb your hair. We will mount a grand exhibition, an opening with great publicity and fanfare. In the hospital, at Dayr al-Salib.

9

Such is the mortal sin: to defy time.

To combat time. To forget and to yield to your own nature. To forget, at any moment, that the morning star (sought by eyes weeping or now extinguished after the final and prolonged struggle, when sleeplessness, pain, or fear has fissured the muddy depths of night-time, eyes vacant and white, abandoned by the beloved and even by the beloved's shadow), to forget that this star—to whom it has often been said and to whom you say now: "O Star, distant and magnificent, light my heart, light my heart just a little, now, and then you may forget me"—that this very star has gone dark. This star was already dead and gone a few thousand years before the Messiah's birth, and what you are looking at now is time past and now lost. It is the light that still pours forth, and by doing so it bridges the distance to your eyes. The other edge of this distance is in darkness; it is the void. Look at yourself, seeing the star that is no more. Then go away and forget.

I look at her. I know it is just a question of time passing. I know that as I take another breath, she begins—at the other end of that thread of distance—to tire of me. How, then, must I word my response when she tells me that she wants to find a job?

Have you begun to get tired of me? No, she will answer me.

"No," she answered me, smiling.

I will not ask her whether it is because I am repulsive.

"Do you need money?" I asked her.

She was silent. She does not want me to give her any money . . . too much of an opening, too likely to plant seeds of power, possession, management. These days, women think; they want a portion for themselves. "A slice of this lovely world to manage, just as you do."

They were once the ones who preserved us from madness and perversion. Now they will act as we do and to hell with what little equilibrium remains in the world. Women will be our true chastisement now. As the Evangelist said, "To he who has will be given and his wealth will be increased." Now they will resemble us that we may see ourselves, just as when a son's growth shows his father his own legacy of genes. Look at me in my disobedience, for I so resemble you that I am your son. Come, let us reap together.

"Fine. But what sort of work will you find when you have no papers? And why would anyone give you work when no one is introducing you around or recommending you? And you don't even want to be known to anyone. Are you going to ride all the way down into the city every day and return? What is it that you want? You're free, do as you like!"

I did not wait for an elaboration. I left the house.

You're free! You're free, do as you like! What does this woman want? Say "You're free! Do as you like!" to any woman, and then you'll see the consequence, a result that she knows to implement only by instinct or nature. You'll see that the whole thing is no more than a game, a pretext to go out, to parade her body in public. To go out and show her self, to see what the possibilities are. One male isn't enough, as long as she is already someone's lover anyway. It isn't so much to have sex as it is to play this little game, to be impulsive and frivolous, to act on her mood. Even if she finds their bodies absolutely disgusting, or even if her own morals constrain her or the memory of her training suddenly leaps up to control her, there are still the eyes. This is the freedom we all will be granted when we go out into public together, when we all crowd into those broad, beautiful, well-lit streets—us, them, and the certain disaster of our resemblance. Festival time!

In the village square I stand beneath a balcony to shield myself from the rain. I watch the ropes of water pouring down in the light coming from the municipality's streetlamp. This evening we have electricity. But many windows remain dark: countless people have returned to the capital. They've put their children into the city schools, but their houses here are kept ready and in good repair so that they can return at the slightest sign of trouble, even though they must know that the village is not secure either, that it has performed its national duty, accepting its share of the fiery battles that nothing can guarantee will not return. But no doubt they also know that all of the regions outside the city pass the wars back and forth; perhaps secretly they're wishing an imaginary security for their own villages and hoping it is someone else's turn, though the choice will not be theirs.

The village square at night in winter: no one is here and nothing moves. But the smells and sounds are not the same now—not even the smells and sounds. The village chimneys no longer send the same vapor spiraling into the village air heavy with moisture. Because the price of fuel—all kinds of fuel—has skyrocketed, folks burn anything in their stoves. They'll pick out whatever they can find that catches fire from all of the things that were harmed or destroyed in the most recent battles: window frames, doors, chairs, shelves, perhaps some of the wood that they still gather from the nearby forests, which have begun to recede. And when the rain falls, the sound it makes is no longer the one I used to hear now that rapid and unplanned construction, which has converged on the roads and narrowed them, has especially congested the square. The populations of cities far from here have been overcome, it seems, by a sudden longing, an abrupt nostalgia: they are stockpiling fresh cement, strong and hard enough not to shudder in a raid or shatter across the ground like the fragile tiles that are nearly gone now and are so horribly high priced anyway. These folks, overwhelmed by their unaccustomed yearning for the past, seem deceived ever so slightly; betrayed in their emotions and savings, they are like a man faced with the unexpected appearance of a former lover whose face he had forgotten, but who now holds him to account.

What entices the dogs to come out on a rainy night? Insomnia perhaps, since dogs do not truly sleep. They just doze and awake with a start, already running to guard something, anything. They don't have the morals that a human sentry would have. They mount guard simply because they don't sleep. They guard unconsciously just because it is their nature and because they're bored.

Male dogs go out at night looking for females, and female dogs for males, so they don't pause at the rain, even to a heavy downpour hurling onto their hot fur and sending the water back as steam. They stand with one leg raised, open their jaws, and bound into the darkness, which does not bother them because they can see what they need to see. And because dogs see what they want to see and pursue it, they feel no fear.

As a child I was afraid of the large square submerged in darkness. Squeezing my father's hand as we crossed in front of the church, I asked him whatever questions came to me just to hear his voice answering. Talk, Father, so that the square will once again look like the daytime place we know well. Talk, Father, so that the cloying heaviness of the night will melt and dissolve to nothing. Or sing your *mawwal* loudly from the top of the sloping alley, to unlock the murky night and detect the walls that guide us home. Louder and then louder, so that the empty depth of the church will recognize you, the images of its saints on their firm strong legs; so that Saint Elias the Living will remain lodged within his icon, our Mar Ilyas, who stamps out the devil all the while glaring at me. Flourishing his grand sword, he is about to bring it down upon the neck of the chief of the heretics, whom he holds by the hair on his head. . . . Papa, do it so that Mar Ilyas the Living, who will return at the end of Time, will not return right now.

The streetlamp goes out. I have stood here a very long time, I know. I am shivering in the chilly air.

Drunk and wet through, I returned to the house. She was not asleep. A towel in her hand, she came to me, asking where I had been all this time. I gave her a fierce shove. She stumbled but regained her balance. She picked up something from the floor, tied back her hair with it and said to me, "Don't you dare do that to me again."

Vomiting into the bidet, I asked myself what she meant by my not doing "that" again. Did she mean that I should not stay out until morning, coming in dripping wet and drunk from a place she did not know, squandering my health and making her stay up all night worrying about me? Or did she mean I should not push her away with my hand?

The bed was warm. "That" would not come again, I told her. She did not pick up the towel to dry my hair; she did not turn toward me. Before I could fall into the deep sleep of total exhaustion, a realization came to me. This woman also had a darkened village square in her life, where the rain falls at night from high above the lamp; and she, too, had a father's voice that grew louder to see her through the dark streets. And many memories, ones I didn't know and over which I had no control—she had those, too. And I recognized that in the years that had passed, I had not been there in her life, and in the years that followed those I had not been there either. It was as if I sat in the eye of the needle perched uncertainly between sympathy and angry resentment, I thought, for I remembered also that it was in those years, and in the other years, that this woman had known a man other than me.

Before I fell into the sleep of fatigue and anger, I put out my hand to touch her forearm. She brushed it away. That was the first time. . . . She refused me.

Before I slipped into a deep sleep in spite of myself, I went running in the village square, making an enormous commotion. I pounded my hooves on the ground, digging into it; I breathed fire from my nostrils, stirring up dust and soil. I was an immense bull, enormously powerful, running and lowing and filling the empty village square to every corner, scraping away its nighttime with my great paired horns, heedless to whether it rained or not.

10

And then the seed germinated, and my woman was gliding away, away.

When I spoke to her now, there was nothing special about the way she listened.

Like a faithful sentry she stands at wait, prepared to read the signs that organize my words into coherent sentences, into thoughts of some use, or of some harm, and of a known logic to which she can respond. Like others, she expects signs rather than meaning. She wants the lucidity that words produce, not the meaning that I produce.

When you speak, you must forget about how others are listening to you, for those others have their own vessels, to which your escaping words cling like magnetized iron filings, there to take the shape of sentences that they send back to you in their responses.

No one hears the lyrics in your voice. No one listens to the music of your larynx or notices the rings of sound your throat makes, rippling outward to spread like flat loaves of bread above you in the sky. No one listens to the lilting sinuousness of your voice as it rises from your windpipe or the bronchi of your lungs, from your dry lips or your trembling palate. They seize your words without grasping the resonant vibrations of your phonemes, and then they formulate the meticulous structure of an answer. They engineer their responses to calculate, to sort, to classify with precision because they are looking for hidden meanings and buried intentions. They're probing for and against . . . against, against. In what you say, they want to figure out what is theirs and might have been in your safekeeping for a long time. They cling tightly to a rope of words that becomes theirs in the moment that its end appears on the tip of your tongue—theirs because the other end is already held between their teeth.

As for what I have to say, I'm perfectly aware that it is all nonsense. Sometimes it's a lie, sometimes an evasion, perhaps an act of duplicity, a sport, just an empty tune. My words tumble out of me to sit placidly beside me: like many other things, they might well be mine, but they are certainly not parts of me. They're like the plate from which I eat or the socks I wear. I talk the way someone else might lift a leg or an arm intending to dance—to fill empty space with movement or commotion, but without any sense of the certain and necessary utility of a law, for instance, that one cannot possibly camouflage or evade. Without that sense of efficacy as inescapable as retribution, as a piece of evidence to be entered in my permanent and eternal trial, or, as we call it, an exchange with others, debate, dialogue, conversation. There is always a shade of competition to it, of struggle, of premeditated murder. Or it is competition in the sense of the compulsion to add something more, to provide a simile, to offer a congruent comparison . . . premeditated murder. Why don't I have the right to turn out words peacefully, naturally, as if they are the substance of an emission that gives my body relief, just as I rid myself of excrement or discharge mucus or exhale carbon dioxide—or musk, if, say, I'm a gazelle rather than a human being? Why don't I have the right to operate the bodily instruments that the Lord granted me, in the manner I desire, without inciting a challenge, a match, or without provoking more suspicion?

I do not want to see her turn into one of those people whom she has begun to resemble. But, for her sake, I do not yield prematurely to my oppressive impotence. Don't hold me responsible or demand an accounting as the others do, I tell her. Listen to my voice and think of me without preconceptions, if you love me. Today I might well tell you something different, something that contradicts what I said yesterday. This, you see, is my ballad, my soul's will to wander and search, to explore the pain of contradictions. To you, therefore, the words I spoke yesterday and today held no meaning. I told you something else, another narrative, one in which yesterday's words contradict today's. It's a narrative of me, not merely thoughts that clash as they're caught in a net of bad intentions. I lied to you, yes, but look at how I've suffered for being a liar: I have had to refute, to evade, to deny . . . I've had to play tricks. It would be the easiest of situations for me not to lie to you. It is easiest for you to catch my flying words, to gather them all and force them together, and then to declare, "That's a lie." The easiest course for you would be to discover a thought that gives the lie to another thought, one utterance that falsifies another. Then you would be just like the others. Then you would see my words—the lies that I make no effort to conceal convincingly—but you would not see me. Delighted at your own cleverness, you would cling fanatically to your own view of things, becoming like all of the others and so failing to love me. And then I will lose you. And I will lose this chance, your chance to love me. And so I will not learn from this; I will gain no exemplary lesson out of it. I will only lie all the more, for I will not resort to silence and restraint. I will let myself go; I will lie with abandon, and my deceptions will thus become ever more skillful. I'll be so good at it that I will deny others the opportunity to enjoy discovering the flaws in my lying. At that point I will offer them my speech that reassures them, that sounds so much like them, that returns us to a dialogue of equals. But I will not offer them my voice. I will not offer my lying mouth, singing the melody that returns to infuse my whole body.

But she did begin to resemble the others. She did hold me to account. And when I attempted to avoid tumbling prematurely into a state of immobility—for her sake—and when I tried to explain my dilemma to her, she peered at my words suspiciously like prey surrounded on three sides and facing traps that are almost certainly set for it on the path ahead.

When, one day, she said to me, "You don't give any weight to what I say, you don't give any importance to the words that pass between us, you want only to have sex with me. A man who doesn't talk to his wife has no respect for her and holds all women in contempt" . . . when she said that to me, I almost burst out crying. She wounded me deeply when she said that; such a complete misunderstanding made me suffer terribly. She didn't understand my amorous feelings at all; she didn't see my passion for her. "All you want is sex with me," she declared another time, and I turned my face away as my eyes filled with tears. Suddenly I was sure that every pore in my body, granted to me by the Lord so I might adore and make love to her, was vanishing now that she had expressed such doubt in me. What misapprehension, that she saw her soul somewhere else and no longer inhabiting her body!

My heart was so anguished that it felt truly split—wounded, cleft in two, causing me palpable physical pain. She was leaving me no choice. She had barred all of the exits; I could not make a move. She was thinking, I knew, that now she had pushed me into a corner, thwarting all of my arguments. She believed she had won this round in the fight she had started, and now she would induce me to acknowledge the error of my ways or at least to reconsider the poor calculations I had made; and after that, she assumed, I would correct my behavior. I would improve. I remained silent, for I could see more errors on the horizon, coming in succession, mounting higher, like waves from the sea.

She had barred all the exits in front of me, and so I made no response, for I could see the coming loss, resplendent in its clarity. It was the loss attendant upon her calculation that her body was elsewhere; that it was her possession alone and that with fierce concentration she could sequester and deny it; and that she would use it against me to separate her own self from it thoroughly, tossing it into the profusion of bodies, others' bodies, indistinguishable, bodies used to wage war and to increase the population.

A sorry loss: she would wage war against me now, and naturally I would not be able to find a place for myself outside of the fighting. She would force me into it to the point where I would honestly choose in its favor; that is what has happened in every war, from ancient times to the present, and will continue into the future. The moment comes when we enter war's time. We lose ourselves to the fight so completely that we must hone our instruments to the utmost perfection . . . until we must meet the final loss, the loss that will return her to this simple and primary truth, simplicity itself, a truism even: that her soul is inside her body and that it is not elsewhere.

This is what I saw: for my tears had blinded me. I saw a certainty that she would not realize without a loss as complete and perfect as this moon, red and full.

Then . . .

The only recourse I had then was to lose the first round, to retreat deliberately and as part of a larger design while hoping for a miracle. I would step back with all the calculation necessary so that she would advance to gain the territory I vacated.

I set about making her believe that I felt a need to speak to her, to talk with her, and that every word she said bore a profound importance that required deep listening, comprehension, and comment. I began to comply with criteria I had formulated for this urgent situation. I gauged precisely how soon I must contradict her flow of words if my listening pose was to appear genuine. I did not agree to everything she said. I made objections, I disputed points, and perhaps I even got slightly angry. I could be as obstinate as a mule refusing to retreat from his miserable, willful stubbornness except when treated very gently and stroked tenderly. I let her stroke me so that she would choose on her own to desire me—to want my body. So that she would take the initiative, would arouse me so that I would sleep with her, while I concocted an elaborate likeness of a man impervious to arousal because his head is so full of thoughts, of the echo of what his heart's beloved has just been saying. . . . I was so successful at this that sometimes I even pushed her away, gently, putting her at a distance so that I could continue responding to what she had said a moment ago, and provoking her to become even more absorbed in her longing for me to the point of trying to silence me. My sadness grew at seeing her so visibly resembling the common run of women, slipping from between my fingers to join such a throng that I knew well. She was becoming lost to my sight in the mass of women's bodies, women with their mouths so prone to lying and invention, their miserable little minds, and their delight at the genius of modern intelligence, the latest products from which waft the odor of plastic packaging applied in mass-production factories, the smell of the belongings of the nouveaux riches. They are the masters of rejection, casting away an object's beauty and value by using it in a way that loses all of its distinguishing character or positively turns that character upside down.

My grief pressed me to want her out of public places.

My grief rescued me from the torment of monitoring her small intelligence. My grief intensified my determination to bring her back inside of my love, to return her to that other soul of hers that she was resolutely working to lose—to bring her back to her original body. I reined in my fury, my lust, and the violence of my desire to condense into a single, forceful deed all that I wanted to say to her. I set myself to meditating on her face, sorry that she could not see it when it glowed for me as it did now. I was sorry that I could not get her to revive her body's own exhaustive memory: to remember the body that had been free, ardent, perfect, and pure, in the moment in which her first egg's first contours were formed; the moment in which the pain of her coming menses flared, though the blood was yet to appear; the moment in which her body knew, before she herself knew, of coming desire. Memories from a time before she heard her body spoken about, before she learned and read and filled her head—from a time before that forgetting of the body and its quiet dropping away from her to unite with other bodies, the other bodies of all other women, there to be lost among the repulsive abundance of a herd. Long before that, for it was in those moments that I fell in love with her. In those moments, she alone, apart from all other women, was my woman.

I restrain the violence of my desire and apply myself to the act of remembering, the attempt at a despairing retrieval of what has departed me. Slowly I peel away her clothes—slowly, so that she has the time to anticipate me, because I do not want her to follow me. I open her own doors for her that she may walk through those doorways herself, leaving herself to come to me.

I slip my hand beneath her clothes and move it from her waist upward to her shoulders. I push her shirt back and pull the sleeves from her arms. I press the heels of my hands into the roundness of her shoulders, and my palms follow their curves, gliding in circular motions, as I gaze into her half-closed eyes. With those lowered eyelids she's like someone trying to regain her memories. When her chest comes forward, I lower my hands to her breasts. I shape my palms into cones that I may sense the cold nipple at each cone's tip; and I send the warm gush of my blood to the still surfaces of my palms, that her nipples might remember the instant when they first broke through the surface of these breasts . . . which now rise by themselves to fill the insides of my hands, pressing hard against them.

I delight in her, and so I forget my grief. I push my body against hers until the whole length of us is pressed together and even our arms all the way to our hands, until we form the shape of a cross, and I can solder the insides of her feet to the exterior of mine. I marvel at how perfectly matched are our heights, our frames. I am just fuller enough to be able to cover her, to keep the cold off her nakedness, and my body brims over her so that I can encircle and surround her entirely.

She is uncomfortable with me, though. When I stay on top of her for any length of time, it bothers her. Her throat produces an affected, choking laugh as she complains that her breathing is constricted and she can't endure the weight of me. But it is only because she has forgotten. She doesn't remember that not so long ago she drew her breaths from my body plentifully enough to fill her lungs.

When she leans toward me and tries to press herself to me, I cross my arms into a barrier, and she understands that now I want to be alone. She thinks I am resting, regaining my breath. How can she not ask, though, why I have changed? Why do I no longer cradle her in my arms, no longer lift her knees and thighs to my body? She does not ask now. And I leave her to go where she wants to be, in public places that harbor no memories.

But as for me: I do remember. I remember the grounds of my passion for her, at the very beginnings of my emergence into life as a tiny embryo in its first months when all of my chromosomes were still female, still XX, before the Y chromosome entered me in my final months of life in my mother's belly and transformed me into a male. Even as a male I swam in the waters of the female womb, and my maleness could not be assumed. I remember what came before my lethal struggle to be a man, before my birth and after it, and then after I reached puberty. But she forgets.

I am the loser, and she forgets that her soul is not elsewhere.

11

Whenever I come out of my amnesia, which attacks me so frequently now, I know that I will not see her again.

Which of the garden's sunny patches would I have seen her in, I ask myself, sitting within a circle where the sun broke through the clouds amidst gray curtains of rain? I walk through the garden to a point opposite my window. I gaze upward, but I do not see my own window. I am never certain about it: Is that square really my window if I don't see myself behind its panes? And the squares look very much alike: from the outside, all of the windows are identical.

I am aware, too, whenever I come back from my recurrent spells of oblivion, that seasons have come and gone. The seasons of the year, following one another in sequence, have passed while I have been away. I know we're in the midst of springtime because there is a great deal of greenery, the air is balmy, and the ground is dry. When I try to step back, to see myself in the previous season, I can't find winter. I find I have forgotten it completely. I guess that probably I spent it exactly as I did the winter before it; and nothing remains of it that I can recall. Nothing of it remains to carry me into the spring that envelops me now.

Whole seasons are blanks to me, but their loss does not sadden me. I suspect that they all have gone by in the same way, quietly and calmly. But what does bother me is the loss of things that I can't identify. I am lacking those things, but I don't know what they are and I don't know where to start looking for them. I don't know if they can be found in objects and belongings that I can see or if they lie inside my body, a lost accessory or need. I am missing things, but I don't know what they are.

That is why sometimes I'll suddenly be on edge: I feel a pressure rising in me, and the urgency of it consumes and exhausts me. I start looking everywhere, along the ground, pacing, searching. I hunt with my eyes first and then start digging with my foot, turning over small rocks, pushing away the dirt. I bend over to pick up fallen leaves and mounds of cottony dust lying against tree trunks. Frantically I tell myself that I'll surely find something. I forget that I am searching for things I need, things I lack. Feverish by now, I tell myself that I will find an object that someone has forgotten. I will find and take for myself something that perhaps fell from them unawares or that they deliberately misplaced and later on replaced with something else. They can always acquire something else. They are not like me—for I know that I will not inherit anything from my family's lives or from their deaths. And no one will give me one of his own belongings, anything he possesses now or once possessed. My craving recurs, my yearning to stumble upon something. My longing returns, again and again, stronger than ever, to drag me behind it, pulling me step by step, setting the rhythm or breaking it, and I move in every direction like a fly darting through the air.

What I secretly want so much is to find a part, a piece of something. I want to find something that is incomplete, deficient. A thing that is incomplete does not belong to anyone, and no one will demand it from me because ownership can't be established unless it is complete and whole, undivided and cohesive. A part, a piece that has been loosened or detached, stripped off or broken or scattered, doesn't belong to anyone. I hope to find a lighter without its flint, a shred from a newspaper, a bulb without its socket. A pen without its plume, a ball that has been punctured and lies flat. I want a ball that has lost its air or has no air nearby to inflate it. I want a ball without its lung or a lung without any air.

Like those who stroll through this immaculate garden, I long to find something that no one will demand from me. I crave this so that I can own it obsessively until I die. This is what happened to Jabir: one day, he found a huge brass bullet casing near the garden wall and refused to give it up. The nurses massed around him, but neither gentle persuasion nor force induced him to let it go. He held it as closely as the light of his own eyes. He fought desperately, his whole body mustered protectively to shield it. "Never!" he was screaming. "It's mine!"

Around him we were screaming, too, encouraging him. "Watch out, Jabir! Don't give them the casing, it is yours!"

We all hoped that he could hang onto the big brass casing, though inside of me something was whispering slyly that one day he would forget about it, and we would be able to pinch it from him. Or so I imagined in my heart of hearts.

But Jabir lost this lovely object of his. They took it away from him in their vicious preying, but also because of their fanaticism, their obsession with cleaning and picking up and emptying. Because they strip us bare of any trinket we happen to like or want to keep. We want to keep it even though we know it is lacking something and has no usefulness to anyone. We choose it for that. We choose it out of our own meekness, our sense of renunciation. We choose it because they have rejected it. It is their refuse, its utility spent—any sort of usefulness it had is gone. Even so, they can't bear to see us with these things. They think we'll get back our health if they strip us of everything, if they create an empty space around us, for us, in us. It reminds me of how Asmaa reacted when I held onto the shiny chocolate bar wrapping that was so bright and colorful. I refused to give it up, and she saw my refusal as proof that I was still an invalid. And the more she tried to convince me to throw it away, telling me it was useless, the more agitated and worried I became. Every time she tried, I became more obstinate about keeping it, more afraid that I would lose it. I got completely absorbed in stroking it, folding it, and creasing its corners to sharpness. I was stunned by her dreadful insistence on throwing it away and asked myself constantly why she had to visit me at all when she spent half of her time with me trying to persuade me to throw away something that was this precious to me. It was so dear to me that I woke up at night, terribly afraid, to search for the shiny green paper on which a brown cow smiled at me from a field of hazelnuts.

I know that I have missed entire seasons, but knowing this does not sadden me. Sometimes, when I am stretched out on one of the wooden benches in the soft and gentle sunshine, staring at my pale and narrow fingernails, I ask myself what it is that I would really like to find in my frenetic search, which wears down my body for hours on end when the desire strikes me as it does, unexpectedly. Rebuking myself, I say that I am still behaving as if the hospital were a transit point rather than a place of residence. And as if some trifling object with a part missing—for which no one has any need—will give me the security of possession: confident ownership akin to a return to the outside world where the beloved and chosen flocks of the Lord reside.

A pail without its handle, without a hand. A hypodermic needle without the needle itself, without a vein. Laces without a shoe, lacking a foot, without a step. A breast without a woman, without its trembling eruption under my hand.

Like milk, like milk.

Like milk, this woman rises in me. Like the milk that rises in the breasts of a nursing mother and spots her garment, her absence rises in me. I search feverishly, looking perhaps for her breast—without her—because I've known, since she left me the first time, that she will not return, she will no longer be. And in her breast's ultimate absence, her hot milk rises in me, gushing from my hands, from my head.

Allah! My God, how did she leave me when she left?

When night fell and the blackness spread and thickened, and still she had not returned to the house, I knew. "It's the heavy shelling," Asmaa said to me. "It's not the darkness that has kept her from returning."

Then Asmaa said to me, "You shouldn't have brought her back by force, that time, on that hot day and at a major checkpoint. She told me what happened. But tonight it's because of the shelling that she won't come back. She will return tomorrow, you'll see."

I wished Asmaa had died along with my mother. I wished Asmaa had died and my mother had stayed alive. Or my father. If only Asmaa could have been the one to die.

And now here I was, sitting on my settee, dwelling on my knowledge that she would not return. That she had left me and gone back to her own folk. The shelling was growing more intense, and my sense of oblivion and loneliness was getting stronger now that Asmaa had left our apartment in the capital to go down to the shelter with our neighbors.

Now, as I sit on my settee, my knowledge of her absence is active. My head drains empty of her, and then my body, and I take in my emptiness like a machine. I process the knowledge of my emptiness to shorten the time, from this point on, that will pass, empty of her. I consume my emptiness like an unstoppable machine.

In my empty head the ringing of a distant telephone finally reaches me, a clear and constant ringing free of the tumult and noise of the bombing. A limpid, faint, yet clear ringing that comes directly to me. A long ringing that does not stop.

I go into the room where the ringing comes from, entering darkness like a sweet dusk. I sit down next to the phone. I raise the receiver.

"Hello," I say. "Hello." I hear the voice of a woman, a stumbling, bewildered voice.

My voice is not his, the woman says. But she is happy to hear me. She says that for many years she has gone on dialing this number and listening to the long rings in the house where the shutters are closed. She knows he has gone away. That he has left his house, closed around its darkness, but she dials the number regularly so that she can see the house in her imagination and revive her memory of its particulars. When she knows that the telephone is ringing inside, she can see that telephone, and everything around it wakes up at the sound of the ringing. She brings back to mind the furnishings, submerged in the darkness that she loves, and she reassures herself of emptiness, of the master's absence. She needs to be sure of this emptiness, needs to touch the absence of that man because it is the only way to remember him. She tells me that the ringing of the telephone makes her a picture, like a photograph that shows the man of the house and his absence simultaneously. And that the pleasure of hearing the ringing is also the pleasure of recalling the number and dialing it like any other number that may ring in the ear of whoever it is one is seeking. "So I dial him, like this," she says to me, "as if he is there. And I practice my ability to recall the number, knowing perfectly well he will not answer when the phone rings to that number. I get pleasure from the ringing that makes the house vibrate, from knowing that my own action has awakened the interior, as if I myself were there.

"Perhaps"—she says—"I feel that way because he left without saying anything to me. I learned about it from the concierge who guards his home from the assaults of squatters made homeless by the fighting. I found out that he had gone away and would not return. Like one who dies without seeing death coming, without even a few seconds' knowledge of its arrival. Those people, they say, stay among us for a long time; they watch with us, beside us, watch for their deaths, and they look upon their deaths. They require much more time than do their loved ones to accept death as true and to bow to it.

"One day I will stop dialing the number and listening to the long rings," says the woman. "I will stop as soon as my desire leaves me and shuts down: that desire I have to ring inside the home, to stir up its stagnant air. That desire to stop seeing the smart furniture that surrounds you. Please, I ask you to plump up the clean sofas on which I will take off my shoes and stretch out, because I like to card their soft cotton as I always have done. I will lift my feet onto the wooden coffee table and push away the rippling crystal statues with the edge of my right foot before I take a long breath, feeling the velvety nap of the silk armchair and how it hollows itself out lightly under my hips."

Part Three

1

When that woman became my home and my family, I knew that I had lost home and family because she would never be either one to me.

A woman who is not from your folk cannot be family. She can only make you lose your family. Her blood exists only for her own memories, and her womb is only for those to come who—with her—will build a home for her. When you knock on the door of that home they have built with her, they will ask who is knocking before they slide the bolt.

She stayed a long time. She stayed until I had lost everything that had been mine.

Since she came to stay, our apartment in the capital is no longer the home that my mother occupied. It no longer looks anything like the place I knew inside out, even with my eyes closed, in the days when I scampered through its corridors and thrown myself into the comfortable chairs. The slight odor I would catch as I climbed the stairs, returning home exhausted and famished, has disappeared completely.

It wasn't that they changed everything overnight. She and Asmaa, I mean. But every time I returned home, I found a new addition or discovered that something had been taken away. This was their way, apparently, of diverting my attention from their takeover of the apartment. It was their way of deceiving me about it, too.

Asmaa became more like *her* sister than like mine. When she saw I was annoyed, she assumed it was because of the money they were spending to play with colors and spaces throughout the apartment when there was no need for it. Asmaa supposed she was simply helping to establish my happiness; in Asmaa's eyes, they were building a nest for my love and establishing my possession so that it would become my home rather than continuing to be the family residence. But she would come to me with pretexts so lame that even the most simple-minded listener would have found it hard to believe her. For instance, she said that the most recent shelling, which had left its traces on our neighbors' apartment and had shattered windowpanes all around, had ripped apart the old curtains in our windows, and now they could not possibly be mended. Or, when the west wall collapsed, exposing the sitting room so that the apartment was open to the street during the time we were in the village, she claimed that it was no longer possible to clean the upholstery on the sitting-room chairs, so the material would have to be replaced, and then she would have to match the new colors with what was already there and buy a new buffet to replace the old one, now ruined, whose wood no carpenter in the world could repair for a reasonable cost.

But, like *her,* Asmaa was a woman, just as primed by nature as *she* was to forget, to replace, to leap from one thing to another, for she knew instinctually that her memory itself worked by substitutions and changes. It does not bother a woman to leave her family, change her name, and go away: she might as well be taking off one dress, putting on another, and going out. Perhaps this is why women have been such successful spies: after all, their roots do not run deep. Perhaps it is because their childhood is always before them, ready to greet them as soon as they give birth.

How could I possibly face the two of them or even try to complain or object? When I saw them putting their heads together and whispering, laughing together in this or that corner of the house, needing only gestures to understand each other, I asked myself, How can Asmaa feel no alarm, seeing the tension and anxiety that *she* shows whenever the bombing quiets down and the streets and crossing points open for those who want to go from one sector of the city to the other? How can Asmaa be sure that this woman will stay, when she has family over there, her own people, a husband, whom perhaps she remembers only when she is in this state of agitation, brought on by her awareness that it might really be possible for her to cross over the line and go to them? And how can Asmaa suppose that this woman really would leave everything she has, intimating that—because she has been cut off from them for so long—she is dead as far as her family is concerned, and that she doesn't even mind, much? Doesn't mind that they believe she is dead, and doesn't have the courage to let them know that she is over here, on this side, and has chosen to stay? For my sake. For me, the person in whose love the pair of them work themselves to death daily as they steal away the very air of the house and its time. The home that was my mother's, the home where I'm obliged to harmonize my movements to a new array and placement of objects, a mean and bastard mixture of things.

Stupid Asmaa rebuked me when I wasn't "agreeable," as she put it. As, for instance, when I refused to help them carry out the old buffet after the doors had been stripped off to make it easier to pick up and to carry down the stairs. I did not give them any help in lugging it over to the empty lot near our building and tossing it onto the heap. For days, I watched it through the windowpanes, under the strong rain. I watched the wood swelling, and then I saw the finish crack and split under the glaring sun. I used to see my face reflected in that finish as I hid beneath our big dining table in an attempt to provoke my mother's alarm or to get her to announce her fear of losing me. She always made as if she were searching for me, anxiously, all over the house, pretending to forget until the very last moment to look under the table where she would find me.

In the end I found the house and their frivolous games boring and irritating. I was going out a lot, leaving the two of them to their own devices now that I knew it was no longer my house. But women know: these wars that force them to desert the streets strengthen them, augmenting their power over the home. And homes that no longer have electricity or running water or have lost part of their structure become theaters more submissive to their authority because then it is easy to rearrange everything, and every alteration has a legitimate excuse behind it. Once the home has become the sole refuge from violence, the women let the men go out as they wish, for they are certain of the men's return, of that primitive need for shelter and protection. The women become more tolerant about letting the leash out as far as the streets and more lax about mounting watch.

I don't understand why it was so, but as my daytime aversion to that woman grew, my nighttime passion for her and my desire for her body became fiercer. I was able to conceal my longing perfectly as long as I was not by her side in bed. But why was I so determined to hide it, to the point of becoming obsessed by the attempt?

Yet all of this remained within its normal and reasonable bounds. It was more an occasion for puzzlement than anything else—before she left me for the first time, when I followed her to the barrier at the crossing point on rue de la Musée and brought her back by force. I knew I would not be able to endure for long the spotlight that her escape had trained on me, those glaring white-hot rays of light that were to become the utmost source of my torment here in the hospital. Perhaps it was my comparison of those two moments in my life that led me to understand why light causes me so much pain and agony. This is what they offer to someone who has a secret that others want. Under those rays they position prisoners of war with their secrets. They torture those prisoners to extract the secret, but it does not come out until they aim that light on them, a light that sterilizes their insides, emptying them completely. Then the torturers can embalm their prisoners. They've put every cell, every enzyme, under the burning rays, to block all defenses: those of yesterday and of tomorrow, those of your life outside and those of your life within. These are the rays of light that suck out all of your warmth and freeze you in place, that freeze things in an icy hue of glittering whiteness. They intend you to float in a void created by the light until its sterilizing power causes you to settle. The light exists to assure that nothing will remain, whether outside or within. The light exists in order that the insane cease their twisting and convulsing and writhing. So that they will be straight and still, parallel to the room's horizontal lines and pacific in its still and sluggish air. So that jailers will turn those who harbor riddles inside out to expose their sheltered secrets, like a leather glove turned inside out whose five fingers poke nakedly and stiffly outward.

The night she escaped I did not sleep. I sat under those rays all night long. In the morning I was there at the crossing before it was scheduled to open at six o'clock. By five o'clock I was in position, lying in wait for her at the side of the only street, the street she would have to come along, one hundred meters before the military barrier. It would be impossible for her to pass without my seeing her. She would not be in a private car. She would have to get out of the service taxi to cross the barrier, to walk the distance of the open space that was reserved for inspections.

I began to wait, working to maintain my composure. I need to stay calm, I told myself. After all, as soon as she sees me, she will come to me. She will put her arm in mine, and we will return together.

Almost all of those crossing were on foot. Only some important people and a few individuals with permits or on special missions were in cars. The occasional automobiles that I saw were luxury models, and they passed quickly.

Farther away, service taxis stopped at distant intersections and disgorged their passengers, ready to ply their return routes. Hoisting their numerous bags and cartons, people plodded off without turning around to look. Armed with identity cards and personal papers, they headed for the control points to await their turns without visible anxiety. Setting down lines of bags and boxes, they took out their documents unhurriedly, uncomplainingly, smiling at the soldiers and civilian officials who did not check anyone very thoroughly. They lifted their many bags and boxes again and walked off in the opposite direction of whichever way they had come. They set down their bags and boxes once before the barrier and once after it, picked them up yet again, and resumed walking with the same calm and easy movements, except that when they crossed to the other sector, their faces suddenly took on the alert and watchful demeanor required by a difficult task or a delicate mission, as if whatever they were about to do— no matter how trivial—would be inescapably thorny. The service taxis allocated the passengers according to destination with an order and precision that seemed to have the force of nature, in thrall to a law in place since long-gone eras and ever repeated with wisdom and monotony that admit no intervening chaos or shortcoming. For one thing, the shape and emptiness of the space through which people must pass in the light of a blazing sun announced its function unmistakably. Unsullied by trees and their shadows or by the shade of nearby buildings, the square would demand, of anyone wanting to paralyze the clockwork operation, far more than the individualistic schemes of a sniper trying to break that time-honored law. The square's configuration stymied every possible opening an adventurous sniper might take advantage of. To stop this operation it would require a shower of missiles and rockets—in other words, the sort of military decision that only a regular army would take and only after an overall assessment based on the study of large maps rolled out on a table around which all the generals are gathered.

The principle of the brightly lit open square as the place of crossing no longer admits the frivolity of chance or the indulgence of chaos, which continue to govern the squares of villages and hamlets.

2

The square was the meeting place that brought together the ringing of the huge brass bells in all three big churches, with their powerful and enormously compassionate patron saints, our lords and fathers who have preserved our blood from the impurity of mixing and the fog of intermingling, from shame and fragmentation. The bells' metallic resonance maintained its pure clarity, for the air coming from the heights that bore the waves of sound gently was dry. It was uncontaminated by humidity that would thicken and clog the vibrations producing that clear sound, perhaps gagging the hypnotic effect of the bells' spreading presence.

Only the clean whiteness of thick snow is visible through the thick darkness of the nighttime that falls heavily in the winters that villages on the heights endure. The darkness that drops early over the thinning yellow rays of the sun hides the patches of gray white that ooze dirty water, after car wheels and children's shoes and men's boots have bruised and mashed the snow there and once the market has done its work, strewing the clean expanse with mud patches, vegetable scraps, peels from fruit already eaten, and overflowing garbage pails. The blood of slaughtered animals and remnants of their dung lie exposed along the facades of the butcher shops, to fade with the sun.

As usual, the municipal streetlamps were dark. Asmaa came up to me, bringing her candle to the window where I stood. Now I could no longer see anything outside, for the candle flame transformed the windowpane into a mirror reflecting the room's interior. I saw her in the glass, too, as she bent low over her feet to pick out the fuzz from her wool socks. I took the candle from Asmaa's hand, blew it out, and turned back to gaze on the square.

I couldn't distinguish anyone in the crowd of men standing in the cold air. I knew they were talking when I saw the masses of steam tumbling from their mouths. Before I returned to my seat next to the coal stove, the ringing of the bells had faded; only one remained, clear and regular. Asmaa said that it was the bell of Our Lady. Tonight mass would be said in her sanctuary.

The faint low voices in the distance were approaching slowly. Soon we could hear well enough to know it was the recitation of the prayers. We could understand the words because they were repeated so frequently: have pity on us. . . . Though Asmaa returned to the window, I did not because I could see the women from where I sat.

The women, their children trailing them, walked through the evening dimness: it was six o'clock, and a dusky light lingered. Against the edges of the street where the snow was still intensely white, the women's wraps seemed a deeper black. Heads bare, they walked behind the icon of the Virgin, carrying lit tapers that created the effect of floating figures who were detached from their lower bodies melting into the darkness and from their bare feet that plunged into the murkiness of the stinging wet surface. As they passed by, chanting their prayers of humble intercession, doors opened on more women, sketching the sign of the cross in the air as they stood on humble thresholds. Others, not so meekly devout and wearing thick leather boots, joined the procession. Before the women had turned into the twisting lanes leading to the square, the men's somber faces were turning to the interior, while children remained on the thresholds, neglecting the bowls of broth going cold inside.

The women pressed on with their chanting as the night slipped farther down over their candles and a cold breeze arose, though it was deflected from the lit candles by the women's protective open palms. Their voices might have picked up slightly as they approached the church, for now the sound of the enormous bell threatened to submerge all else. In the square dominated and almost effaced by the magnitude of the dome of Our Lady—nearly invisible now in the lilac sky—the mass of women and children multiplied, for there they met the prayer processions converging on the square from other directions.

The men, seized by a sort of fear, abandoned the entire square to the women and retreated to press their backs against the walls. A few of them hurried to the bell rope, ready to ring it with whatever strength they could command, as the women knelt and prayers rose.

Here is the scene: Standing alone in the square, Hanna opens her arms and begins to talk to the Virgin without any preliminaries, eschewing chants and formulaic prayers. She requests the Virgin to protect our village and to crush our enemy. In our names, all of us, Hanna makes her requests, for she is our door to the heavens whence sits the throne of our intercessor in her Son's presence. Her chest toward the sky, Hanna asks the Virgin to send sulfur and flame raining down on whosoever threatens the Virgin's children, the Virgin's obedient servants. Hands are raised to heads that are not yet bare, whipping off head coverings that land on the ground if not merely pushing them back. Then the hands descend to chests, baring them so that all hearts will be revealed. The women's powerful fists beat heavily on their exposed chests. The sound rises as if they are drumming on little tablas to the rhythm of the penitence and the insistent piety behind the sentences of Saint Hanna, whose words are coming faster and in fragments. The priest emerges and invites them to come in. Hanna puts her veil back on and leads them inside.

It was Hanna who, after losing her two brothers, began to dance and trill. She refused to let them be buried until the young men of the village had brought two enemy corpses to witness the prayer for the dead and the burial from the edge of the hole dug for her brothers' grave. It was Hanna who came out of her house that night to scream in front of her door, her hands sprinkled with oil.

That night the small roof terraces filled slowly with men who began to fire their guns into the air. Some had the old-fashioned rifles that left exploding puffs of smoke, but others carried the newer machine guns, whose long staccato reverberations interrupted the rising clamor of the bells, their peals blazing across the village like a shower of burning sulfur. But it did not matter. They all fired.

Everyone ran in the direction of Hanna's home, ululating in long screeches of sound. Joy it was, but it came over their faces as terror or excruciating pain. They ran toward Hanna's house, most of them not yet knowing the news, but as if they had no need to hear it. They sensed that a momentous event had descended on their tiny planet, and so they ran. Small kerosene lanterns were showing in doors now left open, and without hesitation they streamed forward, smoothly massing to flow down the way, a dense penumbra of light moving along the rough and narrow slope that ended at Hanna's terrace. They did not need to enter through the small doorway to catch sight of the blue and white statue that was giving off oil.

Some lanterns hastily retraced their path, scrambling up the slope and moving apart in every direction, for now it was vital to return with cotton that would drink in the oil. We would pass it over our aches that we might be absolved.

The Virgin gave off her oil for many days after that one, and all who wanted to make the pilgrimage came. From distant places folks arrived carrying their dry cotton; saturated, it was wrapped and rolled up with all necessary care in waxed paper to prevent its evaporation or leaking. Priests whom no one knew came from afar to say mass under powerful camera lenses in the home of Hanna, whom one saw now but rarely, even in her own home. Some women in our neighborhood said she had traveled to Rome at the pope's request. Other women said that in the frequency of her prostrations and prayers she had neglected to eat and had become so weak and ill that she had been carried off to the hospital. Still others insisted that Hanna was no longer visible even when she was present among us, for the Virgin had claimed her, wanting to speak to her alone. And the Virgin would return her to us, they said, but no one knew when that would be or how it would happen. Even her age seemed no longer to inhabit her body. No one, even friends of her mother or very close neighbors, could remember when Hanna had been born. She was in her twenties, they thought, or perhaps in her forties. Or was she in her fifties?

Hanna no longer spoke to anyone in the village; no one among its folk heard a single functional sentence from her tongue. Her silence seemed to warn of our ever-greater exposure to great peril, or so hinted the men of the village in their terse manner of speaking, their few words always suggesting the necessity of further vigilance, more precautions, and greater preparedness to make sacrifices. They had become all too aware that in these heights they were far removed from the web of towns, from the conditions that governed the capital, and from the talk that circulated there. They knew, too, that the fences penning their flocks in the nearby fields were the securest and farthest borders they had. The infrequent movement of men between their houses and the square, emerging from the narrow alleys, gave no sign of anxiety except when the young men from the militias would suddenly, shockingly, come through.

A few months later Hanna shot from her house once again to scream in the night. But this time no men clambered onto their rooftop terraces to shoot off their guns and no women ululated. Putting their hands to their heads, the women ran, oblivious to the little ones who were still inside their houses or were standing on their thresholds. As if they feared to go too near, people gathered in a circle a few meters away from the screaming figure of Hanna as she stood alone in the night. The villagers who had thought to fetch their kerosene lanterns brought them closer. Close enough to see Hanna's hands, which were raised in their faces as she screamed.

She said to them that the Virgin no longer sprinkled pure oil. Now the oil was tainted, corrupt, for now it was infused with blood.

Blood. Blood.

The Virgin yields blood because what is to come will be terrifying.

She said to them that the kerosene lanterns would no longer give light, nor would the ordinary white candles. All that could drive out the blackness to come would be the honey gold candles, the holy tapers of Jerusalem. When the day of blackness descends without warning, we—in our enslaved humanity—will see nothing; we will not see the fingers on our hands unless we can summon the light of those honey-colored tapers. A great black cloud will come down upon us from the sky, and the sun itself will go into eclipse. The stars of the firmament will vanish, and the Lord's night will be upon us.

The night of the Lord. For the Virgin drips dark red blood with the oil.

Ya Allah, the listeners breathed. God, my God. We must get the honey gold candles of Jerusalem. And so we began the frantic search for the blessed candles until there were no more, even in the most remote villages, although people kept secret their own provisions and sources of supply. Villagers made do with a candle or two among several families living in houses clustered together. After all, the days of retribution would not go on for long.

After they had readied their supply of candles, people sat waiting. They shared predictions. They said the world would end before the next millennium, according to the prophecy whose source no one could clearly pinpoint. The priest warned them to take heed, for the village was in grave danger. He counseled prayer, contrition, and precaution. And so they prayed and they readied their candles and they waited in terror.

Then they started to ask themselves what their sins might have been. They had neglected their devotions, they discovered, in their excessive attention to the affairs of this world. And so their enemies, feeling their own strength, had triumphed. But we are the children of the Virgin, and she will show us her mercy. To most of us she will show mercy, for were it otherwise, she would not have appeared here to offer oil—and blood. The black cloud, someone said then, must be those people they call Somalis or the black people who come from the other side of the world to slay us, the children of the Virgin Maryam. The young women wept, and the older ones scolded them, telling them their tears were useless.

There were not many weapons in the village, and most of those that remained after the young men had taken the useable ones to the front were ancient and primitive. But the men cleaned the guns that they had, groaning and complaining, and put them somewhere close by without saying much about the beauty of their weapons or boasting as they would have done before the Virgin's appearance. No one said very much even when they were at home, and the few visitors to the village remained mostly silent, too.

No one visited us. It did not take Asmaa and me long to learn that people were distrustful of the woman who was with me. And we learned—Asmaa and I—that people wondered why I, a young man, had remained in the house rather than going off to fight for our people as the other hearty youth of my community had done.

I don't remember that she spoke at all throughout that time we spent in the village, the woman who was with me: this woman who had fled with us as the capital emptied of people who were driven away by the long nights of bombing.

What I do remember is that she kept to one spot in the house and rarely left it. And I remember that she did not meet our gaze when we addressed her, Asmaa and me, even though we spoke very little. Whenever Asmaa left the house, she avoided being with me in the same room. When Asmaa returned, she was never in the sitting room. She would leave us alone so that Asmaa could tell me the latest news that was making the rounds, could tell me at her own pace and in her own way and without having to watch her words. We would glance round and find that she was nowhere to be seen. Soon we no longer expected her presence. We no longer called her to sit with us to hear the news, stories we had most often received with sarcasm and mockery when we first settled in the village. Asmaa no longer insisted, either, on inviting her to go for a stroll when the weather was fine. On one occasion Asmaa told me quietly that she worried that our companion would be faced with ugly words. I understood that it was me whom Asmaa was guarding, fearful that someone would accuse the woman accompanying her of being a spy. And one time I remember suspecting that Asmaa was trying to provoke her into saying something bad about her own people so that at least she would seem detached from them.

Sometimes it seemed to me that she was afraid. There were times when I thought she might be crying, when she shut herself all day long in the bedroom or spent hours in the bathroom washing her clothes. But I never surprised her with reddened eyes, not even once, and not even with moist eyelashes. I wondered in surprise and discomfort what her thoughts could be as she kept to her near-complete silence and continued to avoid me. I thought perhaps she regretted coming with us to this remote place that resembled nothing she knew. Or perhaps, I mused, at some point she ceased to love me and is simply waiting for the appropriate moment to leave me and return home.

She was cold whenever I approached her at night, colder than was justified by the wintry chill of the village. Perhaps she knew that I did not come near out of desire for her body, for she seemed to know better than I did those moments that I would feel no desire. She seemed perfectly attuned because she did not even try to convince me that she took pleasure in my closeness. She simply let me move her body as I wished, yielding to my hands. When I pulled her close, she came close. I put her head between my arm and shoulder, taking her icy fingers to my lips to warm them. I raised her face to mine, and she closed her eyes so that she could not see the smile I gave her. She believed I was trying to comfort and reassure her, not to love her. And for my part I detected no desire in myself to make love to her so as to correct her impression. She would remain cold for a long time, and I could not understand why I could find no desire in my body. I think I felt pity for her nakedness when she was that cold, and I knew my body would bring her no warmth. And maybe it was because when she was like this, I saw her more as a child who happened to have large breasts. It saddened me to see her always so cold and grieved me to know that I could not be the father who would warm her in his embrace or the husband who would make love to her. And I would get confused about myself. Who was I, lying next to her, the night outside so very empty, and the snow so white, so immaculate, and so still?

3

Asmaa told me she wanted to stay in the village. And Asmaa stayed.

She said good-bye to Asmaa as if she would not see her again, though in very few words. She picked up her few belongings and stood near me waiting.

When I had told her that we would return to the capital, she made no protest. She did not worry out loud that I might face danger from the shelling that continued, though less intensely. She did not prevaricate, but neither did she show any pleasure, enthusiasm, or impatience to leave. She acted as if she were waiting in a train station and did not worry about spending whatever time she had to spend there. And now here was the train, arriving precisely on schedule. She might as well have been expecting an ordinary, predictable event to take place, and here it was, happening.

The fault wasn't hers. She wasn't responsible for any of it, I told myself again and again in the car. I'm the one who decided to return to the city, and here we are, returning together.

She didn't even glance from the car window at the place she was leaving, the village where she had spent more than a little time. She did not look back toward the cluster of houses, now beginning to shrink and contract as if the snow that cloaked them was squeezing them. She didn't look: it was as if she had never lived there and had not even passed through.

Was the village that was now remote to my gaze, distanced by the glass over which the fog of our breathing swept a film of gray, a source of sadness for me? Or of anger or entrapment, a feeling that I had lived in it longer than I should have? I no longer knew. I knew only that it had become distant, that village, and had shrunk enormously. I also knew that if it had not been for the woman beside me, I would have stayed there or would have left it long before. I knew only that never would I have chosen that particular cold morning. I would not have picked that morning, I knew that much, but I did not know why it did not suit me.

But she had not chosen that morning either. She had not dictated anything to me. I had simply told her that we would leave for the capital, and she had packed her few things and come to stand beside me.

She was a woman without any place, I mused a few days later. And she would not be able to endure any place that was mine. How, I asked myself, would I have viewed my surroundings if I had not been looking partly through her eyes as well as mine? What would things have looked like if I had not been worried about the impact of events on her? I asked myself whether without her presence I would have felt ready to step outside the family mold, to contravene my cousins' habits, eager to separate myself from all of them. Would I have even left the village, when most of its sons and daughters were going in the opposite direction, leaving the city to climb to their natal village with their few remaining possessions?

I had no doubt that a woman's place is wherever her man is. A woman's place is her man. But I was not her man: she proved that later by leaving me. And once she had left me, I became absolutely convinced that I had been foolish to take such heroic stances; my noble and just sentiments, my aversion to fanaticism and violence, looked trivial now. I was nothing but an ass and, furthermore, was a particularly stupid one because before she left me, she had stripped me of my final refuge and my own people—completely, permanently, for I departed still burdened by my own sense of fairness. She knew that she had turned me into a creature no better than a naked worm and one without a family, abandoned in the midst of the turmoil of a battle that we had at least to admit was fratricidal. She left behind a worm that, if killed in the street by a stray bullet, would have no one to go to the hospital morgue to identify it or to carry it to wherever its family had their ancestral mausoleum. That woman took my burial place from me.

Since that morning I have known that something inside of me cracked, that some male hormones were extinguished. Otherwise, how could I be as calm as this, standing near the checkpoint barrier at the entrance to the capital? Why, when the armed militia guy was treating me so contemptuously, did I feel no bitterness, none of the stomach cramps that always gripped me when I was forced into silence and submission because I was so feeble?

"Why isn't a man of your height and weight out working?" the armed man ribbed me. "You aren't working, and you aren't carrying a weapon. So how do you feed your wife? How can you sleep with her? Or does she feed you and f——— . . . you big mule! Is she your wife, anyway? Where are her papers? Get out of the car, both of you."

It was raining lightly. He would not let us take shelter beneath the wide tin roofing that shades them as they search people's belongings. We stayed there for hours. Many and long hours we stayed. The fellow must have forgotten us, for when he turned and saw us there, he made an irritated sign at us that told us to get into our car and out of his sight.

We were dripping so much water that we practically saturated the car seats, and for days afterward the upholstery was soggy. The mere fact that the seats remained damp for so long and the car interior harbored the stench of rot and decay seemed sign enough of my defeat. It didn't occur to me at the time that, had I stayed on in the village, sheltered by the ancestral prestige of my family, no one would have considered treating me as contemptuously as this. Nor was I capable of recognizing that if I had had family members in the car with me, no one would have humiliated me. At the very least I had been brought to the depths of the powerless, and for days I suffered from a recurrence of my customary stomach cramps because I had kept the humiliation, the injustice, pent up inside. At the very least.

She had stripped me bare so that I would be alone before her, so that I would resemble a woman more than a man. Other women. Even the women of my village do not come out like naked worms from their surroundings, their skin; they don't come away from their men. As do other women, those who resemble her, who are frightened and alone.

Then she left me.

Twice.

When it happened the second time, Asmaa insisted that she would come back. But, said Asmaa, I should not have used force. I should not have brought her back from the crossing point at the museum when she left me the first time. That is what Asmaa said.

I was on the pavement, staring at the pedestrians who were crossing. I knew that she would show up that morning to cross to the other sector during the hours when people were allowed to cross. As soon as she caught sight of me waiting for her, I believed, she would turn toward me. I thought that was what she would do when she saw the regret in my eyes, spanning all the moments for which she wanted my contrition, everything I was aware of and things I wasn't aware of that might or might not have mustered my remorse.

But that is not what she did. When she caught sight of me at the side of the road, she quickened her pace and continued to walk toward the barrier. I was truly astonished. I called her. I called her by name and turned in her direction. She began to run without having even turned to look at me. Everyone noticed—the soldiers, civilian officials, pedestrians—because the smooth, regular process of crossing through the checkpoint allowed no gesture that might break its rhythm or disturb its orderly tempo, which was as strictly controlled as the beating of a heart. I found myself running, too, running toward her, as if I meant to prevent her from running or to deter a bullet that might stop her crazy progress. Then everyone began to stare at me as well. She was a few meters from the soldiers standing at the barrier and was still running. To them, and in flight from me. I was well aware that she was running from me. I heard the sounds of guns near us: trained on her and on me. "Stop her!" I yelled to the soldier. "That woman wants to escape."

She came to an abrupt stop at the barrier. I was still several meters away. Everyone stopped what they were doing and watched the two of us.

"I want to cross," she said to the soldier. "My home is over there, and this man kidnapped me." As if I couldn't hear, couldn't understand. By now I had reached the soldier. I asked him what this woman had been saying. The soldier demanded my documents, and I gave him my identity papers.

"This is my wife. She's trying to escape, to go to her lover."

"This man kidnapped me, and I want to go back to my family. I can give you their names, and you can contact them."

The soldier led us to a nearby tent in the square next to the hippodrome. He requested her papers. Requested them from her. "She isn't carrying papers," I told him, "because she intended to escape." I demanded to speak to him alone, and we walked away from the tent. I begged him to understand my situation and to avoid causing me further scandal. She was my wife and wanted to escape to where her lover waited over in the other half of the city. "What would I do with a woman, why would I kidnap her?" I asked him. I told him that I was a professor at a certain school, a well-known one that had been de-molished in the bombardment. I told him I was not armed and did not kidnap women. I named some distant relatives among the militia leadership. I offered to describe some distinct markings on her body. "You know what comes over women sometimes," I said to him. "You know how they can behave in order to make our lives hell."

"Take your wife and go home," he said. "And God help you."

I walked over to where she waited. I grabbed her hair, wrapped it firmly around my wrist, and said, "Come on—we're going home." She gave the soldier a frightened glance, but she didn't try to fight me. She followed me with a submissiveness that surprised me. But I didn't let go of her hair. I pushed her inside of the car and slammed the door. I waited before getting in to see if she would try to open the door on her side and escape again, but she didn't attempt it.

The power was out, and the elevator was not working. She climbed the stairs of her own accord and as if nothing out of the or-dinary had happened. I opened the door, and she went in, breathing heavily. She sat down. I remained standing and stared at her. She sat absolutely still, staring straight ahead at the wall. Absolutely still. Straight ahead at the wall opposite her chair. And I stared at her.

I suddenly felt very, very tired. My knees seemed barely able to sup-port me. Perhaps it was because she was very pale or perhaps because I was so immediately sure that she had not succeeded in fleeing, that she was here, opposite me. Perhaps it was because she was a woman who really wasn't very pretty at all. And perhaps it was because I had hit her.

My God. She is much stronger than I could have imagined. She has extraordinary endurance, outlasting me, and she can put me into a state of weakness and fragility that I will find it insupportable to sub-mit to and impossible to stay in.

Miserable fellow. A poor fellow, I am. I kept repeating those words to myself, tears pouring from my eyes. A poor fellow, I am.

4

It is the television channel broadcast from her part of the city. I tune the television to that channel from the other sector so that she will realize that I have no objection at all to watching it together, and so she'll understand that I did not choose to live over here: that this is our place, the two of us, at present. She will not live over there, I want her to see, because (after all) I am here, and there is no difference between here and there. Both live one set of circumstances. One hell. And so if she wants to think that everyone has their own hell in which they'd rather be scalded, then she has the television screen. She has the channel from the other sector that she can watch however and whenever she chooses. And we can watch it together.

We flip among the many channels like acrobats or like butterflies flitting among the varied flavors of the nectar of hatred. There's the sugary, honeyed one, anyway: such are our daily vitamins that revitalize the sap of life within us, pushing us forward to a new day. To a deep and healthy sleep like the one we trustingly resorted to in the arms of our parents, then to a new and blessed morning in which the Lord's sun looks down upon us with its light and warmth. The sun of the Lord whose light and warmth are no longer as strong as the light of our belief—a belief as incandescent as the Symtex that hides in booby-trapped cars.

All programming is interrupted immediately if he is to appear. When he dictates his message to us, though, he has already left us behind. He's looking at his own image on the videotape along with us, and his pure, saintly soul witnesses his body along with us. We all but make room for his spirit between us on the sofa as we listen to him on television telling us, "I am the martyr." We're almost persuaded to look around for him as he delivers the message that he himself wrote. At the moment when we see him and listen to him, says the script, he will already have become a martyr. At the moment in which we see him for the first time in our lives, his life will be over. We have come to recognize him the moment he appears, gazing down upon us out of a poor recording and the lurid colors of the video. There he is, one of them—the saints of the video, who tremble only on our television screens and in front of their inconsequential videocams that are so technologically primitive they give no weight to the image.

How can that form bear any weight when it is the spirit that speaks to you now, the soul without its body? These are sainthood's baby chicks, hatched by the machineries of tiny nations whose only power is to detonate those images, to explode the form. These are the ones whose mothers, even, have forgotten them and who have bartered their vigorous, youthful bodies for the clamor of antennae.

And he barters us. He smiles as if directing his warm countenance to the waves of megahertz, as if we are our own screens and the magnetic vibrations that produce him. As if we are the planar glass of it: he speaks to us and then to his own clan, and only then does he thank the party or the organization that showed him the way. This Path of his now appears uncannily akin to those scenes painted on cardboard where the road begins at the front of the stage and rises on the backdrop, doubling back and winding until it dwindles and disappears in the sky amidst cottony blue clouds as dancers and singers heighten the billows of their steps, their voices surging to the heights of their soprano range.

He makes like our grandfather, teaching us Life through the dark, severe nights. He instructs us on the ruin Life brings, on its poisonous bitterness. He warns us that there is no warding these things off, no deflecting their ultimate blow. His smiling face will not suffer us to err as we walk the path of knowledge. This is the final lesson. This is the lesson that allows no review, no corrections or changes, the lesson that time and its wisdom can only confirm as unshakably certain.

As if he has repeated these lessons to us for so long that now they roll easily off the tongue. He never stumbles over a word, never hesitates or stops to think. His smile never vanishes, even momentarily to allow him to concentrate, to collect his thoughts, or to review his memory. Even the seeming effort to connect one sentence with the next does not dampen his smile, as if what he is saying cannot be serious at all.

Did they edit this film before shipping a cassette to the television station, erasing anything that suggested confusion, hesitation, or loss of memory? Or did he, perhaps, write out the message in huge letters before—from a distance—he began to recite them?

When he speaks to us, he is sitting behind a desk. The scene gives gravity and an official cast to what he says. But none of it goes with his smile or with the compact organization of his words, which come out studied, clipped, and exaggeratedly ordinary. Except for certain overused stylistic turns, he speaks like a civil servant, the sort of talk that keeps the wheel of life turning in its slow and humdrum way. These are not the words of someone who has come to disturb life's equilibrium even for a few disruptive seconds. The little theatricals of death that he has prepared seem crafted for the benefit of life and not to oppose it. It's only in the first few moments of his appearance that the faultlines are visible to us.

It's as if he is the spirit who addresses us to say that the martyr who speaks to the people and the nation is not a pure spirit alone. Like any one of us would do, he is speaking to his own family. He apologizes to his mother for not having said good-bye and for failing to seek her acquiescence. He's the boy whom we all dream about, as fathers and mothers, for he separates himself from the crowd, from the throng of young militants, his comrades, who include us in their maltreatment, their plunder and killing. He has become our only child, every parent's prodigal son, beloved of his clan, the stray sheep who returns to the fold.

He tells us that he will shed his blood for us, but when we see him for the first time, his blood has already been burned to ashes and smoke, his blood that is the most elemental condition of our beatitude. His radiant smile illuminates a circle whose glow reaches several kilometers, and the echo of laughter lingers. The blood that so immediately and directly yields such vivid happiness is nothing like the sort that runs through the dark and enclosed tunnels of human veins, blood that goes congested with fear and infection in the joints; blood that induces clots and the menstrual flow; blood that resembles tiny pulsing balloons under the microscope; blood that is analyzed, labeled, and classified; blood that carries nutritional stuffs to and from the liver and oxygen in and out of the lungs.

This is another blood, open to the air, pure, pulsing its way, complete in its compound elements. Luminous matter, this blood has no color in itself, for it is what fixes all the colors of History, what corrects the course of its fluids, what revises the ways of its oppressive, obdurate, harshly compelling geography.

He said to them: Take, eat. This is my body. And they took it and ate. He said to them: Take, drink. This is my blood. And they took it and drank.

As if everything that he said and did was not metaphor, nor was it allegory. They recorded everything on videotape and stored all of it on cassettes. They gave it all to a skilled and clever driver. They told him to distribute copies to every television and radio building and then to the foreign news bureaus. And come back, he was told, before the beer warms up and hatred of the enemy cools down, and before our fellow parties contact us to negotiate over the production of videocassettes.

The poor fellow! The little one, the orphan, the cheated and duped. We might see to make a place for him among us—almost. We might look out of our windows just in time to catch a glimpse of his soul in its swift flight upward, perhaps a glimmer of a tiny meteor that we know will be extinguished the moment it tumbles into our sight. We all but see it among us, there on the sofa: his smile, apologizing for not having shared in our meager evening broth.

But he is not among us, neither beforehand nor afterward. There is not even a grave that those who were once family can visit. He has no place now, outside of the videotape (which will run only once). His place is the air—that which trembles over the poorly colored image, the metaphor and the abstraction. It is a metaphor that conveys no referent, transfers no meaning; it is an abstraction without any concrete notion to bear it.

Did he know that public time, like him, would resort to video-tape? Or that in this naïve, romantic nostalgia that appears to come from some very distant past he is more modern, more fully contemporary, than is our own time—than are we? As if he knew, unaccountably, that our image is our future; to be precise, it is what will take the place of us. The meaning to come is but the image of that meaning emptied of its kernel. The screen on which the videotape unrolls will elevate the authority of the eye over that of the brain. The pure form, the image that the eye plays upon, will be present when we are not; it will be our master. Image of synthesis and hologram, virtual image, created, crafted icon. Absolute perfection. Abstraction in its most splendid trappings, for it has been liberated from the weight of its earliest, primary imperfections. It is the world of exemplar, idea, and image, presaged by the ancient philosophers who died for having craved it. And we, too, were to expend our lives in the grip of its longing, in our lack, for as we are born, we forget. We spend our insubstantial lives reviewing images of what we used to know, representations of the essence of things. Now we will have the essence, made complete. The image, the essence made complete in compensation for the incompleteness of the original. The hologram—a lightness cut away from matter, weight, meaning. Space, to compensate for the gravity of substance.

Nostalgia that seeps from a time long past invades videotape as if it knows that the image has become the decisive factor in these wars, that the enemies no longer come from behind the borders. They no longer mobilize their legions behind the mountains and back of the rivers, at the trenches dug by the spades of young soldiers with water flasks hung on their hips, next to photographs of girlfriends and wives. They no longer cross wide plains, plunging into captured territories as they raise their weapons.

Place is no longer divided into what lies in front of the border and what lies behind it because place has become pure image. In wars of the interior, place falls away. Place loses its stability to move like a hologram, like people now without their places, in the brilliantly lit terrain of combat.

This woman whose gaze lingers on the fingers of her hands reconfirms her own emptiness every evening, and so do I. Now, as the two of us have become the image of our places, we have come to resemble each other very closely as if we're a pair of siblings, brothers or sisters. Looking at her face, I tell myself how greatly she has come to look like me and how much I look like her. Like a married couple who have emptied their lives of the outside world and now pass the hours—long hours—at home opposite one another, their fluids and smells intermingling night after long night; they can't help looking more and more alike. Two people who no longer maintain any borders between them, who are as emptied of place as place is emptied of them. They resemble each other more than their children resemble them because the child moves away from his parents, whereas they move only toward what they already are.

We look so much alike, she and I, when we stand in front of the mirror. And when we face each other. We look so much alike because we have no place beyond this.

Even her body is no longer a place for me.

5

We look so much alike. It is as if the wrath and prejudice of the Lord have drawn our countenances toward each other inside this hospital, here in the place where we have come together after leaving our own places behind, leaving all of those whom we once resembled before any of us came to this place.

It is not the serums and pills they pass out to us that cast this protective veil over our eyes, releasing us from the need to guard our own steady vision when our faces relax, heads reposing on our chests or bent; yet the pupils of our eyes tremble and shift, unwilling to settle or to fix their gaze. Our eyes are reluctant to return to the horizontal position that they knew before. They want to forget that pose, to forget the desire to meet level eyes, straight gazes, those eyes we once hoped to have, hoped before coming here and then despaired.

Our tongues always grow heavy in our mouths. Our lips, which for some time have found it hard to form letter shapes and so now have abandoned speech altogether, can no longer support our tongues or keep them inside where they belong. Our tongues, heavy in our mouths, swell and spill over, dribbling tepid saliva from mouths long dry . . . we've tried to swallow it. No use.

It's as if our limp postures, our sagging heads, give us almost a family resemblance, as if a single mother gave birth to all of us, whom she still lovingly tends, raising us under her protective wing in the knowledge that we will never grow too big or too old for her, will never leave her alone to venture into the vast, wide world outside. And there's the same milk, always in orange and green plastic cups.

But we aren't in detention camps. These are places we've gotten to know well, and we understand there is no alternative to them. The people in them are not hard or cruel and the work they do doesn't manifest the harshness of professions in the outside world. They know us and accept us as we are; they don't attempt to deny us our pains and our fatigue. They don't try to correct our flawed ways. They spend a lot of energy and worry on us and talk about us continuously and with sympathy. They say that we are victims. Their victims, the fingers that point to their crimes, their cruelty. In us they find the compensation that they know they deserve for working with us. They are recompensed for us through us, and when we listen to them, we feel the delight of a person hearing himself speak a foreign language that he never learned in his life. It's as if we are a rare substance that allows them to regain memories of civil communities that have been destroyed or have vanished. As if we are the last civilians, the only civilians, for we no longer have the wherewithal to bear arms, and we never will. Nor are we capable of joining one of the warring parties even if it's a matter of standing alongside our own clans.

We seem the only individuals who still exist, the only bodies that sustain a buoyant presence, floating over the sky of the city like a single atmospheric layer that protects it from the fatal pull of the distant void. With our dangling tongues and our tremulous eyes we are like their only chance. We are the single rope that still anchors this earth to lessen the fierce pull of neurosis and the attraction of escaping that sensible regulatory rhythm of the twenty-four-hour rotation keeping us in harmony with the cosmos. We might as well be the medicine that preserves sanity, the preventive remedy against a madness of extremes: we keep the temperature moderate so that it will not freeze and shatter or burn and disintegrate into tiny, floating particles.

We, who have lost our reason, compensate and comfort them, who see our loss of sanity and measure it against the reason they have retained.

We are all alike in our bodies' abandonment of us, while our eyes—reluctant to see—shun the light and evade clarity. We are all alike as our bodies leave us in favor of dwindling until they are featherweight and very thin and their regular habits have given way to caprice. We don't like to sleep at night, but rather to sing like the crickets nearby in the woods. We don't like to get up in the morning light either; we'd rather curl up, huddle in our beds under the warm covers like squirrels.

We are all alike as we have left our sex behind. We do not understand why they keep us away from women, why they put each sex in its own ward, or how they make any connection between the remnants of our desires and the bodies of women. We do not understand why they cannot seem to realize how lonely our bodies are, how severed and alone, or to see that our desire—if it wells up at all—is nothing but a game. It's a matter of pure play that does not distinguish losing from winning, a beginning from an end. Perhaps because we have lost our sense of even the most elementary features of our bodies, we are like people who have a toy that is incomplete. The sight of women sets off a search through our memories, a search for something distant but specific of which we have preserved only an indistinct, elusive aroma that we cannot enclose in our drawers and cabinets that are always open to the breeze. We don't understand why it is that our presence seems to stir up feelings of fear, almost, or disgust whenever we move our fingers lightly over our sex or handle it, hoping that maybe it will yield a memory of something . . . something of which we still preserve that indistinct aroma that we cannot maintain or revive in the ancient machinery of our bodies. But that does not torment us as it does them. It seems to shoot some bitter aftertaste into their memory.

When our bodies are all alike in showing they have transcended their sex—like lustrous halos above the saints—we remind them of their ancient intercessors or of the ancestors so far away in their remote villages, whose wars were more akin to fencing matches, horsemanship, and the training of country mules into obedience. Those were the men who preserved the purity of the seed, for they carried their members in sacs of tanned hide and presented them to the women as noble dowries.

We, who do not fight in these wars, have no sex to offer to our women. The women passed us by when we left our tribes without deserving the inheritance they offered. We did not seize the ropes that the ancestors threw to us in the gloomy cycle of the generations when, to gain maturity and win the bodies of women, we should have. We should have held on, and firmly; we should have followed the strand that would have led us out of the mazelike corridors of our adolescent bodies.

We did not inherit our knowledge. We did not inherit our members in huge wooden chests along with deeds of possession, the cloaks of tribal elders, and venerable polished daggers. That is why our women disappear in the first puff of breeze or in the moment we go outside to search for the livestock who have wandered off in the late afternoon mists.

We lose our women. They leave us as my woman left me. She left me, twice.

But I knew, the first time she left, it was by force that I got her back. And I knew that she would leave me a second time because she had already left me once. I knew that her first betrayal of me would repeat itself. I knew that what she was doing to me, as her power intensified and my weakness grew, was to make me lose my virility, to expel me from my body and from all the places that were mine.

She expelled me and forced me to stay outside, naked to the open air. I look at my body but can't reach far enough to touch it. I circle round it, but can come no closer, as if I'm having one of those dreams where we see our homes in the distance, lights blazing in the night, but we can't get there, we can't go inside. Attempting to get home, we take roads that we are discovering for the first time, and so we know that these are roads other than the ones that lead home. And home stays in the distance; all the windows are brightly lit, but the house is locked. Our voices do not carry that far even if we shout at the top of our lungs. Then we forget home; we plunge into those by-ways and are engrossed in getting to know them. The cares of the road preoccupy us, the roads that lead there and that we have begun to know so well that we are certain they no longer lead there. And the house grows more and more distant while the fear and the longing for it grow to their most insistent pitch. So it was with my body, as my fear and my craving—for the elusive house, for her—grew to their most insistent, their unbearably insistent, pitch.

6

It was all because I no longer sensed my life to be essential. I no longer felt I had any capacity or force. And so my need to regain both capacity and force grew immense, frighteningly so. I had to be essential to someone. Essential enough to erase the capacity to do without me.

But what I possessed was very little. What did I have to offer her so that she would not be able to do without me? What was within my ability to provide for her when she, every day, saw how little I possess and how greatly all that I did possess could be dispensed with, easily, quickly, without any regrets?

How was it possible for me to keep her with me, to keep her from leaving me a second time, an inevitable second time that loomed close ahead?

She never went out. She was always near me, always within reach. Though she was the woman who had already left me once, it seemed she was always trying to refute the accusation. True, it was an accusation that I never got so far as to formulate actually, but it was always there, suspended between us like a hanged person; and however or wherever we moved, we barely avoided colliding with those yellowish feet hanging precisely at eye level. I did not doubt that she knew the thoughts that, in my anxious state, captivated my head and my heart. And whenever I woke up in the middle of the night, I would find her sitting up, next to me in bed, staring at me in the darkness. Or did it just appear that way to me? It confused and bothered me, when I went to sleep, to know that she watched so intently. What was she observing? Was she tenderly watching the troubled sleep of the man she loved, or was she—like an ever-wakeful witch— submerging my being in evil thoughts, exploiting my weakness as I slept, using my lack of ability to resist her? What did she see in my sleep that I could not see, what was there that I did not know about myself? What was she seeing that I did not see?

Staying in the house and neglecting her appearance were her ways of reassuring me. Occasionally I was arrested by how much she had changed. She was always in a nightgown or in one of those shapeless baggy dresses of faded color whose purpose is to announce that they are extremely cheap and have the sole function of covering the body.

She always wore a pair of my old slippers. Too large for her feet and ugly anyway, they revealed the neglected state of her lower limbs. Her toenails were always clipped and clean, but her calves had lost their warm moistness; they were layered with a thin crust of broken skin, calloused and white, and the sprouting hair gave them the appearance of adolescent boys' legs.

Did she want to show me her renunciation of all that might lie beyond my bounds? Or was she doing everything she could to quell my desire for her body, which instead had increased insanely? It was as if the biological time clock that regulates men's bodies had broken in me, so its clock hands now spun crazily in both directions.

Her neglected appearance did not lessen my desire in any way. Was that because she was coming to resemble those women in my family on whose irrepressibly erupting bodies I had focused my emerging adolescent desires? Was it because she had abandoned the silhouette of those elegant foreign women of whom we once dreamed, though as soon as we were able to bend one of them to our desires, we quenched that thirst and promptly forgot? Or was it that her form, distancing her now from those foreign women, was such a strong intimation of her proximity to me and of her ever-present readiness to accept me because she was mine and no one else's, no other man among all of the men out there?

If that was so, then why did I get so very jealous? She didn't see anyone, she didn't go out; and despite my certain knowledge that her looks had deteriorated, it took only the vegetable vendor's drawing out his sentence a bit as he met her eyes for such an intense irritation to take hold of me that it would positively overwhelm my body. I wasn't jealous in the way I imagine most men feel jealousy—that is, as a result of imagining anything is possible between men and women, in the belief that women are enigmatic creatures enticed by the possibility of provoking desire and sowing discord, that their heads can't resist the temptation of passion and the tricks of cunning men. I didn't feel that kind of jealousy. What put me in agony was to see men looking at her as a woman, even if she herself felt nothing. It tormented me that they saw her as just one woman among many, all of whom were the same, and that they set her within a collective space where imagination plays freely and caprice has its way. That they found her desirable or pretty or even simply refined and nice—as a woman. That they saw in her a woman, and that their slimy imaginations produced images and fantasies. For I know them—men. I know how they cut the bodies of women into separate parts that hang on hooks over their beds whether in darkness or in the light. Nothing deters them from possessing a woman once they have decided that they want her. But she is not a woman who was made, as are other women, to satisfy men's appetites.

The wild stallion that was my jealousy also reared back, taking me into the past, covetous of the life her body had already had and resentful of whatever had not included me. Perhaps it was because she was not my wife. But how can any husband in the world vouchsafe that his wife is really his when she was not so in the past and when there is no guarantee that in future she will be?

I was equally jealous of women's attentions to her, though. I didn't like it when the neighbors talked to her. And I didn't like it when she enjoyed hearing a song or watching a good-looking television actor. But how could I accept or admit this enormous weakness of mine, which I was trying constantly to suppress, embarrassed at its emergence? Yet she seemed to sense my feelings and always drew back from anything that stimulated my jealousy before I could even voice a demand. It was because she loved me, I told myself, happy with this explanation. But it was never long before my doubts rose again, convincing me that she was emptying my quiver of all its arrows just to see what I would or could do then. She was humoring me, keeping abreast of these malign demands and desires, to gauge my limits: At what point would I rest content, free of the anxiety that must have been visible to her, the torment of which she knew?

Later, though, I recognized that she had been giving me everything I wanted so that I would stay away from her. So that I would leave her in peace. So that at least I would cease to torment her.

I knew I was tormenting her, but I didn't know how. And I didn't know why she didn't say anything to me. You are tormenting me, so stop!

Time after time I told her that I was surely wronging her, but that I didn't know the exact nature or extent of my injustice. I returned many times, when speaking to her, to the day on which I had brought her back by force from the checkpoint after acting in collusion with the soldier at the barrier. I apologized to her, profusely and repeatedly, and told her that she was free to go whenever she wanted. I was not bluffing, either. But, saying these things, I truly felt that my humility and my feebleness deserved from her nothing other than acceptance of my apology and a readiness to forget that it had happened.

"Never mind," she would say to me. "Let's forget the whole story. It happened because you loved me so much."

But deep inside I sensed that her response was no more than a temporary accommodation designed to avoid any return to a subject about which I had raised difficult questions. Why did you want to run away and leave me?

Once she did answer. "Because we can't . . . because I thought we couldn't be together, to go on like this." Although I urged her to tell me what she meant, she didn't add a single word of explanation. "You know what I'm talking about," she said, and that was all.

She hasn't left me, then, because she still loves me. But I knew— just as she did—that I would not let her go even if she tried. And she knew—just as I did—that this feebleness of mine distressed me. She endured it with me, as if the two of us, together, were inescapably saddled, afflicted even, with the burden that was me.

In my extreme bewilderment, what other course did I have? What, other than the expanse of her body, which (I was sure) told no lies? Her body, the life raft that would lift me into the air again, to breathe, if it did not abandon me, sending me to the bottom, to those black depths known to me only as the space of her rejection.

My heart was so fearful that it forced me to approach her with the firmest and most determined of gestures. I proclaimed my desire loudly, to forestall her, to beat her to the punch, to cut off any leeway for her refusal or even hesitation. Hastily I swept my mind clean of any likelihood but that she would join me in bliss. I convinced myself that the splendid force of my desire was not to be deflected or rejected, that its vast fury tolerated nothing but pleasure, gratification, and further arousal. I could not fathom how she could remain so still, so rigid, or how after a moment she could look away, look far away. It was as though all that surrounded and composed me had no location, no substance. Perhaps, I would tell myself, she is playing the tease; perhaps she wants to jog my memory, to make me reprise some nasty command I had thrown at her during the day and then had willfully forgotten. I didn't trouble myself for long to recall it, merely trying with my hands and my warm mouth to apologize for whatever the misstep had been.

How is it, though, that the body we love so fervently becomes chastisement, retaliation, a devious body that punishes us? And that she can continue to deny herself to me—as if I can have everything I want except her. She forces me to recognize that her spirit is elsewhere and that it is up to me, as if I'm a hero as legendary as Clever Hasan of the folk stories, to cross the seven seas, to advance puzzle by puzzle, and to decipher each one until I've found her lost spirit in the magic chest. But what chest? You are here; you are in front of me. That's what I've tried to say to her. You are here, and I am suffocating under my passion and desire. Why do I not use my body well? Why do I shed it for you without reckoning my loss, without even caring? Why, after you have abandoned me, after you have had every intent of fleeing from me, just a door slammed in one's face, just a sudden, transient episode that can interrupt life but momentarily—why, after all of this, does the very same day find my head resting heavy on your belly, sobbing, as if cast this moment from the guillotine?

I never know whether she will refuse or accept me. Sometimes it has seemed to me that she is standing before me with a lump of sugar: whenever I am nice, like a performing bear, she rewards me—though it hurts when I strike it just right. And sometimes I have been able to be nice all day long, like a gentle bear, performing my tricks well. Smiling, applauding. Sensitive and perceptive—meek, even. But then, when night comes, she turns me down. Other times I've been depressed, bitter, and as rough and crude as a mule; I have reacted obstinately to everything and stamped my hooves on the ground all day long, stirring up dust, emitting my awful smells to poison the air. And then, at night, she has drawn me close.

I did not always get it right, and I couldn't control or overcome the accumulating hurts and sense of loss. It was not a matter of understanding things in such a way that I could benefit or draw lessons for the future.

She accepted me sometimes. And there were times when she came to me when I did not expect it and was not looking for it. She would press her body against me in the kitchen or when I was standing at the sink, shaving. I would drop everything; I was not slow to take her in my arms and to comply with whatever she seemed to want. Even at times when I was ill, I celebrated her desire as if I wanted to demonstrate how excellent it was, in hopes that she would stop pushing me away when I yielded to a magnificent, unstoppable desire that far surpassed those rare and modest desires of hers.

But her modest desires dwindled even further, until she no longer accepted me at all.

7

"It's because we're no longer good at anything," Jabir said. "No good at war and no good at fucking women. That's why they are interested in us here and why they don't insist on getting money from our folks. Now we are the state's responsibility because once again we've become its noncombatant children."

Jabir is saying he doesn't want to go back now. These days, he claims, he has begun to feign his illness so that he can stay here with us. He loves it that the state has assumed responsibility for him, with all tender and loving care, and that the state doesn't force him to earn his own bread. "I'm no longer of any use to my family and my clan because not only am I not turning out my children's bread, but I'm also incapable of carrying a machine gun even to guard the neighborhood. More important, my wife's body heats up their sympathy! And mine, too. Just one lonely vagina abandoned to the open skies. I repudiated her and I've come back. While she cried, I laughed. My older brother said, 'Take him back to that place, and God help him! God help us.' And so, as you see, I left and I'm ready to enjoy the fullness of my good fortune, my felicity in divorce."

He made me laugh, Jabir did. We chortled together like a pair of ogres. We would shriek with laughter until they came and scolded us because our laughter was too loud. It was too loud: it would wake the dozing hornets in our fellow patients' heads, and they would get just as excited as the hornets.

8

When I'm not sniffing at her like a puppy, I don't see her. I no longer see her when she is not in front of me or when she withdraws to huddle on top of her shrouded resentment toward me.

When she crouches over her submerged anger, she does not disappear from my sight or leave me for an inner room. No. She starts to treat me with watchful compassion as if I am a whale on the verge of extinction. The last of his species—and here he is, in the final stages of his willed disappearance.

She treats me so very nicely to get me to come out of my isolation. To get me to transport myself to a place more like the places that others inhabit, the spaces she sees and imagines. She speaks to me—I am well aware of it—in the manner adults speak to children and animals. Small children whom one cannot otherwise deflect from their stubbornness and stupidity, who do not respond to simple punishment, and who in their stupidity are not only harming themselves, but beginning to destroy the belongings of others. She treats me gently to pacify me, like an animal, so that I will stop howling and biting myself.

I allow myself to be pacified so that she will go away. I take my time in organizing my revenge. In scheduling the lessons of lost love for her. She pleads with me gently as if I'm her little sister. As if I am not a man.

In my corner I hold still and remain quiet. I don't react. I stare straight ahead, swing one leg over the other, breathe regularly and audibly so she will believe that I have settled and calmed down.

When I am not on top of her, I cannot see her. I do not see her because she has pulled herself inside of her hidden hatred of me, withdrawing into an anger like that of the few seconds just before a baby animal's mother decides to kill the infant who is weak or sick or to abandon him out in the open, in the forest, where he will die of illness and hunger while she goes on, his healthy siblings bounding around her teats as they all move away.

When she has pulled herself inside of her buried hatred of me, I know that I am a suckling animal, one with teeth, with molars, but who cannot sever the rotting umbilical cord that I drag behind me. From the corner of my eye I peek surreptitiously at her pale hand draped on the back of the sofa, and from inside of me a heavy sobbing wells up, for in the space between that serene and nearby hand and my lips, she sits waiting like a dragon.

I take a deep breath and turn my gaze away. But her hand moves in front of my open lips as if it is severed and two little wings are bearing it upward. I'm seized by self-pity: poor me who does not have the necessary humility to endure.

I feel as if I am seeing the microscopic strands that make up my nerves twisting round themselves and going dark. I think I am seeing the tendons that rope together my joints contract suddenly to hold themselves tense like wires that cut incisions on the bones. It's as if I see in front of me the pores of my skin, opening wide like little sucking mouths. And I tell myself: I won't beat her. She won't push me to that, to beating her. I'll go out into this night of wars and walk beneath the bombs so that she'll worry about me. So that she'll fear my death. I'll stay out there until she fears my death, until she gives free rein to her desire that I die. I tell myself: I'll go to another woman, one who will love me and die for my fragrance. A woman who will love me, who will utter a cry of joy when she sees me through the little glass eye in her door. Who will nourish herself on the dream of my coming to her in the moments when I'm not otherwise occupied, when I'm bored or irritated or feel a playful desire for change. For a little revenge on that woman who has pulled herself inside of her shell, between herself and her body, like a foolish dragon.

I'll go in to that other woman smiling, bringing with me my pleasant and well-tamed self. Like a true knight of old, I'll be accompanied by that second of mine. I'll drink my first glass all the while looking at her. I'll flirt with her expertly, using the tactics known to other men and women who are connoisseurs of flirting. I'll leave her enough space for her own caprices so that she can tease and pamper me while I do the same for her. I'll devote my attention to her completely, as the famous lovers of ancient times did. For her sake I'll take on the likeness of an actor, one of those dignified, good-looking men who inhabit stories. The other woman shines for me like a distant breach of pure color in the blue sky. For me she adopts the likeness of her beloved and blessed sex. And I follow and obey her desire like a servant perfecting his vocation. I obey her, and I follow the thread of her desires like a savant of maps and their tracery. I survey and shape and handle her along the contours of her demands, and perhaps I even forget myself for the sake of her incandescence, which lies between my hands and beneath me. I am pure and faithful in my sex, undulating with its pleasure, at rest within it as if I am the most finely crafted heir to all of my male ancestors—as if with me they have reached perfection, attained the ultimate form, to close the circle of their performance.

Afterward I do not wash myself, and I do not stay all night. I promise the other woman that I will return soon. I kiss her hands in gratitude but refuse to wash and then to stay through the night. I don't sleep at her place, ever: as if an urgent duty summons me, as if this small wave that begins rising and collecting in my belly as soon as I've closed the door behind me is warning me that its accumulating rush will not wait long. I must hurry away before the first tiny threads of dawn appear, and I return.

I return swiftly. I return as if gunpowder has been lit behind me. I return carrying my own rancid smell and the odor of the other woman, both smells obvious and rotund. I find her in the bedroom. As I come in, she is either sleeping or feigning sleep; either way, she is claiming that she does not worry about me—outside, in this night of wars—and she is declaring, insisting, that she is not binding me to her or keeping me from other women. Her sleeping angers me; her pretense at sleeping angers me. I stand in the gloom looking at her calmly and trying to swallow the anger that rises all the more as she goes on sleeping or pretending to sleep. As if I have not come. As if I did not go out in the first place.

I stare at her head, which is turned on the pillow so that her face is buried. I stare at the implacable stillness of her head. I stare at her curled-up position, her childlike pose, the way she rolls herself up precisely, inside the covers that she wraps around her body as if they are a bag tied around her neck. I stare at her and I recognize my agony, my disaster. I see the source of my grief. This woman is not a woman; but this woman is not a man. My woman does not belong to either sex, so I cannot set about depositing her into the proper archive where she'll be preserved and I'll be relieved of the burden of her.

If it were otherwise, how could she be so self-sufficient? How could she enclose herself within her solitude so completely?

I yank the covers off and throw them to the floor. She does not turn toward me. How long can I remain in such need? How long can I stand my need for her to move, to turn over? How long can I remain unsure, confused, and then humiliated? Why can't you be a woman who stands screaming "Where were you?" in the night? Why don't you grow jealous of other women? Why don't you worry when I am outside, when I am inside the wars in the streets, why don't you worry and then envelop me in charms to protect me from stray bullets? Who do you have besides me? Are you leaving me the freedom of orphans or the freedom of men? If I am a man, why am I not your man?

Standing in our room in the darkness, I tell myself it's the alcohol; it isn't really an ache to burst into tears.

I grab her by her hair and make her sit up in bed. She opens her eyes but does not look at me. It's a curse . . . such hardness. I switch on the light and take off my clothes. I raise her ugly shift. I pry apart her knees by force; she doesn't resist. She puts her hand up to the button over the bed and turns out the light. No: I want to see. And I want to see that you can see. I want to see that you see that I see all of the folds that you want to hide from my eyes, all that you refuse me. I want you to see that I see that you have a sex. That you are a woman whose man I am.

She presses her arm over her eyes, and I slap her. Open your eyes.

Open all that you have closed and accept me. Don't stay still, there. Don't turn away; don't leave; don't make any protests or excuses. Do everything my desires dictate to you. For you I will devise strange, perverse, sick, unexpected desires. And then I will see what you do.

I see a gluey trickle glistening at each temple. Evil befall you! And God's curses. It is too late! Much too late: the time, all time, has passed. I fall. Fall, as I fall into her when I enter her by force. As if my only force is my heaviness that falls, whether I choose or no, from this great height.

I am wounded. I am like an injured wolf as I howl above her. And before I have come out of her I find myself hoping for a quick death that will fall on me like an angel, that will storm my heart, snatch it away, and circle far above, a mere blink of the eye.

So that I will not cry and in the moment just before tears, I pound at her. I rain blows on her, and she clings to me. I push her away and strike like a blind man; she presses herself to me with all of her strength. She tries, then, to force my head toward her body. She picks herself up from the floor, toward me, and embraces me. She knows, then, and she sees everything. A nightmare of hell! I grab her by her hair and knock her head against the tiling. She slips her hand between her head and the tiles to keep her head from splitting open. She doesn't scream or moan; then she still doesn't scream. She doesn't call out, "Stop!" It dawns on me that she doesn't want anyone to hear us. Or to see us. She doesn't want anyone to see me. She doesn't want me to have to take her to the hospital. She doesn't want witnesses whose shadows will later torment me. She doesn't want scandal to touch me. She wants to protect me.

I tell myself she is the devil, and I lunge. I beat her, on and on, until my hands are weak with pain, my body is exhausted, and I have become completely empty.

I go to sleep.

9

I no longer see my father in my dreams. I no longer see my father so that he might teach me.

In my dreams I used to see my father. He appeared extraordinarily tall and large, as if he had abandoned his diminutive self when he left us, in death. I no longer spoke to him, except in my dreams, where I spoke only to him. Father, I would say, my heart holds a hard sadness, round and hard like a stone. He would lay his palm on my chest, and the stone would grow soft. Father, I would say to him, I am miserable because I have lost my red wooden top. Remember, my father would say to me then. Remember, you were hiding it from Asmaa's eyes. You hid it inside your wool sock. In the morning there was my top, spinning and making its accustomed drone on the tile floor.

In my dreams I no longer saw my father, who might instruct me. My father might teach me how a man mollifies a woman who is upset. It is as if, of all that has become lost to me, my father is the one whom I lost this time. How, then, can I secure the father I need if I am to find my own father again?

That is why my questions have remained suspended, there in the sunshine and the breeze. I can see my questions in the distance, like garments hanging on a laundry line in a village whose inhabitants left it long ago after their houses collapsed suddenly and completely, falling in the manner of small children.

How can I console her when I know that my remorse and my avowals of guilt make no difference to her? Or to me, for I know also that my remorse will certainly vanish as the daytime sun drops below the horizon. I start repeating it to myself: all of the women on earth, I say, dream of a man who desires them this much. They must, because they concoct the most amazing designs for that purpose. Even if she never becomes that lover, no woman can ignore such overwhelming desire because it is what is responsible for making her fall in love, even if only for reasons of vanity. It is out of the question not to love someone who loves us so vastly. Otherwise, would we ever love anyone?

How can I give her contentment when I have not the means to offer her anything? When I can grant her no pleasure because I grow jealous of every pleasure of hers, except one—the pleasure of eating?

Without a word I go into the kitchen. I set about fashioning a grand surprise. I prepare tasty dishes for her that I know she loves. I relax, and my mood changes completely as I immerse myself in cooking. Washing vegetables, selecting the good ones. Mincing the onions, melting *samna*. Peeling, frying, grilling. Though I am not adept or nimble, and though my movements are crude, I whistle and sing as if it's a holiday feast, as if I'm inviting her to a grand party. I croon refrains that come surging into my head, though I have no idea how and from where I memorized them. Songs of the popular sort that conjure the names of their young singers and that I know, without having to see it myself, bring her laughter.

I set the table and call her in to eat in a voice that sings with all of my readiness to make amends. To make it up to her by erasing and forgetting, as if none of it ever happened. She comes in, sits down, and starts to eat.

She would eat a lot, but I would urge her to eat even more. I would not let her plate get empty, and she ate with a relish that spurred me to refill her plate. It made me so happy to watch her eat all these quantities, perhaps because her healthy eating reassured me that she was sound. It reassured me of her strength and her power of endurance, and to see her eat like this surely restored my confidence that she was not miserable with me. Unhappy women who do not love their men are anorexic and pale. I saw her getting fatter, growing fat and round and losing her flowing shape. But someone who loves a woman the way I love her no longer cares very much about her figure. Or did her obesity please me because it put distance between her and the voraciousness of other men? My appetite for her, though, remained enormous and was still growing.

But she used to eat a lot without taking much pleasure in the food, as if the more she ate, the less was her enjoyment. So it was hardly surprising that I would not succeed in making her content or in erasing my sins by feeding her.

And so at night I returned to that same brutal attempt, like a new trial that I approached with fear. But I hid my fright, as if this were to be another first trial. I would come back to her, to satisfy her, by giving her the only pleasure I still had.

10

I should not have repossessed her by force, taken her from the check-point barrier when she tried to return to her family that day. That is what Asmaa said to me. "But don't worry. I am sure that she is just late getting back tonight because of the bombing."

This time, the second time, I did not go after her to get her back because I was so sure she would return on her own.

One day I said to Jabir, as he lay comfortably in the sunshine, "Did you know, Jabir, that a person's soul doesn't leave his body through the mouth? If it did, how would someone who is being smothered ever die?"

"True," replied Jabir. "But then where does a person's soul come out?"

"People used to believe—and they still believe—that a person's soul would leave through the mouth," I said, "because the mouth is the most obvious exit, the one that's least likely to stir up any alarm and the most honorable one because it is the instrument of speech and prayer. And because when the soul does leave the body, it must not leave any physical traces behind.

"But a person's soul gets out through the 'door of the body,' the anus, not because it is a door and offers an exit, but rather because it leaves a real trace—even if we were to agree for the sake of argument that this sort of trace is not in the soul's nature. When someone is in his final struggle and everyone is hovering around and then they see that he has let one out, they avert their faces. Now they're certain that he has left them for good. The women can start to wail."

"Ugh," said Jabir, looking upset. "Might as well be dogs. Ugh."

"But a person's soul leaves through his sex, too, and at the same time," I said. "One last shudder, and it leaves a trace exactly like the one that, in the very beginning, inside his mother's egg, summoned him to come down, to be welcomed as a person among us. It is as if the whole of life turns on these two orifices: one for eating and one for love."

"Ugh," Jabir said.

"And love might switch, from loving a woman to loving God—and music. One opening for the body and one for the soul."

"Fine," said Jabir. "Then I still have a chance to see what that shudder is like when I die."

We laughed and laughed, rolling on the green grass. We laughed until they came and shut us up.

But in my room I thought about how seriously I had meant what I said to that fool Jabir. That a person's soul, which entered through his father's sex and leaves through his own, stays on. It's there the whole time.

11

She will come back. Because I raised her soul and shed many tears for her sake, she will return. It is as though this pain we have suffered, that we have applied ourselves to sculpt and polish until it has taken on the light of precious crystal, now splinters, and the image of ourselves that we see in it is spoiled, after we have been apart for such a very long time.

She will come back because we must complete what we have started. Because nothing, ever, happens only once and for all, she will return. Things must repeat themselves, or they will be spoiled irretrievably and destroyed.

On their remote mountains, there is a community of Indians who bury their dead twice. When someone dies, they carry him home just as he is; they don't wash him or change his clothes. They wrap him in a clean white bedsheet and take him to the family crypt. Each family has a single burial place that looks like a tiny house. They shut the door of the crypt behind him and weep all night long. In the morning they go back to their own pursuits. But the knowledge of death and the burial of the body do not persuade the loving hearts of his family that he is truly no longer among them. And the absence of certainty is true suffering. The absence of certainty is the constant longing to see him again. It is as if our mourned ones are not dead unless and until they have died a second time, an occasion for which we have prepared ourselves so that death does not come and snatch them away unawares and does not snatch away our happiness with them.

After the moon travels one full cycle following the death, marking the time that has passed, the family returns to the tomb. They take out their loved one, still wrapped in the sheet, and they say their goodbyes. Then they return him to the crypt. They burn the body in silence and remove the bones. They cull the bones carefully and wash them thoroughly as they weep. They place the cleaned bones in a jar that will be set back into the tomb alongside the jars that hold the bones of ancestors and siblings. They do not reflect on or try to manage their grief until they have buried him twice. Only after the second burial is he really dead, and then their legitimate mourning begins. And then they can remember him, after their tears are spent, through the evenings' fill of captivating tales.

12

"That man kidnapped me twice," she will say.

"The first time I fell in love and followed him. The second time he took my soul, my spirit . . . I thought it was at liberty, unbound, free to slip away. I thought it was elsewhere."

When she dies, her soul will hold itself erect, vertical over her inert body, and it will tell her where it made its exit. Why, then, is it only as we reach puberty that our knowledge of death begins? How—and why—is it that from their very first passion young boys with their dreadful pimpled faces, their eyes reflecting the gaze of prisoners in transport to remote islands, stare toward the opposite bank where they will always see that black cavity like the eye of a storm, the object of their farthest, latest, most tender longing? That first love is like a first taste of death, and they will long rehearse it, that ultimate of pleasures.

She will come back because I peeled her soul like a piece of ripe fruit. I taught her that life is something less than the enjoyment of two bodies; the touch of other men will seem a mere repetition. I taught her to ascend, I taught her to rise beyond, when I ruptured the movement of her hormones and gave her, at a woman's age, the clean, clean body of a little girl. And I taught her how the body rises through abstraction until it shuts its spirit, denies it to the filthy touch of men reprising a single, unique agony to which she is no stranger. So that she can lock her soul away, the spirit that no one can touch but from this place.

Her soul will reach far, far within, to ascend, to exalt itself, to glow in its radiance.

13

When she walks in the street, they will follow her as if she is a magnet that attracts them, the mad ones and the saints and those for whom death is near, unable to resist the magnetism of her space.

At the stations where she stops, her beam will cast its moving, discriminating shimmer, to gather to her light those who—though they stand among the crowd—have begun to move forward on a layer of air packed down by their torments. Their eyes and their breaths will arc in the direction of her glow as if they are live green plants.

Because her star will be light as an angel, she will absorb the shadow waves of their bemused souls and they will recognize her among the thousands. They will turn toward her to look into her eyes. To look into her eyes . . . and the addict will tell her that he suffers pain but that now he bears his own sufferings. Thus, when she is near will madness attain its ultimate contours. When the insane see her, their madness will subside like waters that settle just before they are to pour into the sea, leaving their froth at the mouths of those waterways.

Those whose bodies sense death's approach seek her that they may fall near her hands. That she may touch them and they will depart accompanied by the image of her face. That they may remember her sweet and gentle light.

They will recognize my woman from among thousands because she is so very like them and so very unlike them, because she is among them, yet is never with them. They fall beneath the heaviness of flesh that has been theirs for so long, that they may commit to her the scanty salt that burns when she is near, and their bones may erupt in a flame of phosphorus rather than rot slowly away, their glow extinguished. Enamored of her, they emerge from their small cemeteries; consumed by fire, they die twice, like all noble lovers who never bring things to their resolution.

Because the animals are serene with her and the raving dog is quiet when she passes, watching her and nuzzling his head into the dirt, she cannot be mine only. She must be for all of them because she is not for any one. So that her presence gives a savor to the angels, so that the angels exist, and we are confident that the heaviness we lovers bear offers a hope of lightness. So we know that there exists a sainted intercessor for our sufferings.

14

But she had to come back.

She had to come back, and I had to kill her so that the crazed and the saints and those near death could follow the path laid out for them in the emptiness that chaos creates. For this is ever the way of our suspended lives. No justice awaits our ears, not even at the moment in which our souls will depart from their two orifices, leaving their traces, which, let us admit, are not those thought to be characteristic of a soul. I had to kill her because one woman is not enough, and the exception to the rule is the utmost suffering of the rule. And because every woman we love is an exception to the rule as much as she is the rule's most extreme torment.

Because the rule was made for those who grow old slowly until their light dies out, and it was also made for those who are broken in the wars unawares, without knowledge that death is upon them, suddenly, like a rain whose sound we abruptly hear behind the window although it has long been pelting down. We can hear it only as we cease our pleasant conversation, as the evening's visitors are on the threshold of our good-byes.

Because the rule was not made for those who die of love, for those who perish of suffering and their yearning for weightlessness and light and the imagined silhouette of the beloved. Because the rule was made for those who lay on stretchers in the corridors outside the emergency rooms of government hospitals—for those who stumbled as they tried to walk, entangled in their days and in their melancholy insomnia among the buses.

It was made for those who are lined up on their stretchers in a daze, for those who sink not into a coma but rather into a bout of questioning about what has stopped their machinery from working. Unconscious, they see their bodies as distant, strange, and complicated machines. They ask themselves not only where they are, but also what all of this is as they point in fright to the machinery that is them.

So the gaze that their family is accustomed to seeing in them dwindles and the original one returns, the one that is dazed, searching for the start of their bodies. As if the gaze they turn on us, the vacant gaze, is turned inward and there it becomes full.

It was made for them, the rule. For these sound and straight creatures of the Lord, the terrifying numbers of them who are lined up, joined, colliding, who lie on clean beds and on hospital stretchers. And the suffering of the rule is us: those weighed down by burdens, the mad, the saints of phosphorus, the rabid dogs, the lovers, and the failed killers. And it is her.

Epilogue

I know that a long time has passed during my stay here.

I know that I am tired and that my mind is unwell. That is why, sometimes when I return from my many spells of amnesia, I believe that I did not kill her, that I did not kill anyone. That my sick mind, as it fragmented, was leaping inside my head, escaping as its whims told it.

Perhaps that woman I used to see standing in a circle of sunlight, sitting motionless in the garden below my window, never did exist. Perhaps I composed her from the parts of many women I have known, in an attempt to fill the emptiness in my body with desire. The doctor here is always telling me, in his slimy and insinuating way, that my many doubts are completely unjustified.

One day I told the doctor that I would very likely get well. And that I will recognize the sign of my recovery: I will be able to walk through the hospital or even the garden, eyes closed, without careening into anything or anyone. And that I will see the borders of things but not the things themselves, the gestures and movements of people but not the people themselves; and I will be nimble at avoiding what I need to avoid.

I did not kill her, perhaps. I doubt very strongly that I seized her head and banged it against the rock until it split open and she died. I doubt that my body is capable of that; also, I find the idea of it disgusting. She was not even there when I came down that rough stretch,